Ireland, along with France, Russia, and the U. S., has a habit of producing great short story writers. O'Faolain, O'Connor, O'Flaherty and McLaverty are appreciated by an ever-widening audience here and abroad. Their reputations are secure.

With this first selection of his stories to be published in America, Daniel Corkery is proposed for membership in this select company. His talents are many, his artistry is supreme.

What McLaverty has done for the people of Ulster, and O'Flaherty for the Aran Islanders, this retired schoolmaster of Cork City does for those who till the fields of his native Munster and sail the seven seas from her ports. He knows his people and their countryside and does not sentimentalize.

"Mr. Corkery's art has always been mature," says the *Times Literary Supplement* (London). "Here is to be found an implicit philosophy of life, a sense of continuity in character and setting, a grave pity and understanding by which the bitterness of human nature is resolved. Synge discovered the larger rhythms of Irish idiomatic speech; Mr. Corkery has developed the inward modulation and quieter cadence of idiom; and style and subject express one another — every character is informed and molded by local circumstance and experience, and in every character we touch those moral values which uplift life, however humble or hard."

From the sixty-two stories which comprise his four published volumes, sixteen which we consider to be among his very best have been selected for this collection.

BOOKS BY DANIEL CORKERY

The Hidden Ireland
Synge and Anglo-Irish Literature
The Threshold of Quiet

Short Stories

A Munster Twilight
The Hounds of Banba
The Stormy Hills
Earth Out of Earth

Daniel Corkery

The WAGER *and*
OTHER STORIES

Illustrated with wood engravings by
ELIZABETH RIVERS

THE DEVIN-ADAIR COMPANY · NEW YORK · 1950

CONTENTS

The Wager

....

I

THE gentry weren't broken out of the country at that time; and some of them, most of them, did what they liked with us. When they were beginning to go down the hill, when the old times were gone, many of them had to content themselves with living in their own places, instead of in Dublin or London, and as often as they grew weary of the hunting, the dancing, the cards, would have to think of new pastimes for themselves.

At that time our sleeping place was a long loft over the workmen's sheds, over the smith's shop, the wheelwright's shop, and the weaver's. The weaver, though he was almost blind with old age and had a hump on his back, still gave no thought to anything except his trade. For hundreds of years, it was said, his people had been weavers; and he was terrified that he might lose some of the secrets they had left him. He was a bad sleeper, and any night at all we might hear him getting up and dressing himself and going down to his shop. "Very well, so; very well, so," we'd hear him repeating to himself as he rose, just as if he had been reluctantly compelled to accept the challenge of some voice within his brain —the voice of dead and gone Considines; and hours after his rising we might wake up again and hear the timbers of his machine luffing and swinging about and creaking, not loud and sharp at all, but drowsily in the stillness of the night.

Now, the last thing I remember that night was Sean O'Brosnan turning over noisily in his truckle bed, making its frame-work creak all over. "Between them and him," he said, "there's no knowing night from day." That night the Master had great company at the house, and we could hear them carousing and singing and breaking the glasses, although the full depth of the courtyard lay between us and the back of the mansion. As Sean said these words I was lazily watching the beams from the weaver's lantern striking up from the workshop beneath, striking up through the joints of the flooring, and nosing their way into the cobwebs under the rafters as if they would get at the sleepy spiders. That's the last thing I remember—Sean twisting and turning and snarling both at the weaver and the Master. And 'twould be hard to blame him, for he had given all that day to training the Master's racers, the two-year olds—on the sands beneath the cliffs, a kind of work that leaves one sore enough and tired enough. My work that day had been snagging turnips in the sun, and a half field of them still remained to be done—easy work if the weather held; and I was not greatly put out either by the chorusing or the weaving: my limbs were tired—thick and heavy, and I was happy enough staring like that up at the beams of light ferreting their way into the cobwebs while the pull and drag of the loom went on drowsily below. I went to sleep, and I awoke to hear somebody trying to undo the door of the loft. I thought at first that it was the weaver coming up to bed after working off his fit; but the fumbling continued rather violently, noisily, so I lifted myself on the point of my elbow saying, "That's queer; that's not Peadar Considine at all," because I knew that Peadar, after his sixty years of handling it, could unfasten the rickety old contraption in his sleep. As I listened the door gave way suddenly, and in came the Master. It was a thing he had never done before. He stood there with his lantern raised almost as high as his mouth trying to find out the lie of the place. He did not know which of the nine beds held the man he was looking for. There were only six of us there at that moment: the two horse boys, the two jockeys, a labouring man who was a widower, and myself. The weaver was below in his shop, and the two herds were gathering the cattle for the fair in Dingle. 'Twas for Sean O'Brosnan, one of his jockeys, the best of them, he was looking; and he stood there, with his hunting coat still on him, swinging about, swaying, steadying himself, pouting out his heavy lips stupidly, his limbs still drunk but his mind struggling and struggling to master them. I do not know how it came into my head that it was Sean he wanted:

"Sean, Sean," I whispered across to him, "'tis you he's looking for." Sean was fast asleep, but even so, at my first word he was as bright as day. He sat up at once like a stag nosing the wind. He was that sort, a whisper would go through him, limbs and brain. He was thin and angular and had a lot of high-tempered steel in him; he was the Master's favourite, and he'd win a race or lose it as pleased himself.

"What? What?" he said, staring crossly at me, thinking maybe that he had found it hard enough to get to sleep that night. I jerked with my thumb towards the door:

"'Tis the Master," I said.

Sean stared in that direction:

"Is it me you're wanting, sir?" he said, with curiosity.

The Master couldn't easily find the voice; at last his eyes rested on Sean sitting upright. "Don't rise," he said thickly, and with that he came and sat on Sean's box at the foot of the trestle, and put the lantern on the floor, its light blazing up at Sean's face. It was a long, firm face, without a wisp of waste flesh on it. We felt it our duty to turn away. I thought of it first and the others followed my lead. 'Twas then the Master heard the luffing and creaking of the loom below: "For God's sake, what's that?" he asked, and we overheard Sean telling him 'twas a common thing with the weaver to rise up and give a few hours in the calm of the night to his trade. The Master, we understood, gave no further thought to it. The two of them then began whispering together: it reminded us of priest and penitent; but after some time we noticed Sir Timothy's voice had become a cajoling whine while Sean's grew harder and harder: "No," he'd say, "No," or "Let him," or "What's that to me?" and at last we heard him taking refuge in: "We don't live twice, nobody lives twice."

They were after forgetting all about us; likely for the two of them at that moment the world was a blank about them. "Then I'm broke so, I'm broken out entirely," the Master cried at last; and he took a step closer and put his blob of a hand on Sean's shoulder, as we learned after, and the whispering began again. "We don't live twice," was still Sean's unvarying answer. At last the Master grabbed viciously at the lantern and rose up: "I'm deceived in you, Sean O'Brosnan, I'm deceived," he snarled, and was turning away when a new thought struck him, for he looked down solemnly at Sean and said, "There are Brosnans—there are Brosnans above in Kilvreeda and they'd do it for me—if only I could rouse them," and he kept staring at Sean, we felt, for there wasn't a sound to be heard.

What did he mean by it? Kilvreeda is that bit of a graveyard above on the hill, and what he meant was that Sean was not as good a bit of stuff as his forebears. When we caught the words we were hard put to it to keep from turning towards Sean to see how he'd take it. He made no reply. What we heard was the poor daft weaver down below, and his working, we noticed, had neither quickened nor slowed down; it was as regular as a clock that might keep time forever.

While we still waited for a sound from one or the other in swung the door again, this time with a swish, a clatter, as if now it was broken from the hinges entirely. In the opening we saw a second lantern swinging to and fro, gaily, recklessly. Old Sir Daniel O'Keeffe it was we saw there; and his

five wild nephews, crowded behind him, were laughing and
backing him obedient to his beck and call as usual. It was
with him our Master was after making the wager. Sir Daniel
was jubilant; he was making a sort of sing-song of Sir Timothy, he was oh, oh-ing and ah, ah-ing and "Now, Sir Timothy, now, Sir Timothy," as if he could think of nothing else.
He held that he had won, that Sean had refused the jumping.
He blurted out then, "You're right, Sean," although Sean
had not spoken at all. "You're right, there's a good many of
them in it," he meant in the graveyard, "but not a man of
them all would even try it, would even try it. There's not a
Brosnan in Kilvreeda would try it, no, nor even in——" And
now, look you, how pride and confidence will bring a man
to his ruin. He was sure he had won the wager, the heaviest
Sir Timothy had ever laid: people said afterwards it was all
the land beyond the river—and he couldn't content himself
with that nor with belittling the Brosnans in Kilvreeda, without going back to belittle the Brosnans in the Abbey in Kil-
larney. What he said was: "There's not a Brosnan in Kilvreeda
would jump it, no, nor in Muckross!"

At that we all sat up, hiding our heads no longer. We
looked at Sean. You will remember there is a great difference
between the Brosnans who lie in Kilvreeda and those in
Muckross Abbey. You might say 'tis only since yesterday,
since they came down in the world, that the Brosnans are
satisfied to lie in Kilvreeda. The Brosnans who lie in Kilvreeda were just poor common people like ourselves, but the
ancient Brosnans, from time immemorial they had been laid
in the Abbey with the MacCarthys, the O'Sullivans, the
O'Donoghues, and the MacGillicuddys. Well, Sir Daniel had
the great foolishness to say that even the ancient O'Brosnans in the Abbey wouldn't dare the jump in the wager!
The last word wasn't out of his mouth when Sean himself
was standing on the floor, fronting him, like a vision that was
going to blast him.

"Without going back at all to them that's in the Abbey

there's a Brosnan left here to jump it or drown in the boiling sea," he said, and he turned to Sir Timothy and "Is it now?" he asked him, civilly and respectfully. But Sir Timothy was frightened by that word, the boiling sea, and Sir Daniel was no better; he was swinging his lantern no longer, and his face was blank and cold. "Is it now?" Sean asked again, looking from one to the other; and when Sir Daniel nodded, he began at once clutching quickly at his clothes to dress himself; and at once we all rose up in silence and began doing the same.

II

Here we are on the heights: Look northwards now. To the right, making forward along the fall of the land, you can spy out the trace of the old road: follow it on and on and you'll find it stops suddenly at the edge of the cliff. In the old times, in that place, the rocks fell, making in one single night the ledge that's there to this day. It is about seventeen feet below the edge, sheer down below it; and is, it may be, twelve feet wide at the widest, a rocky bracket of irregular shape. Well, the wager was that Sean was to ride one of the Master's hunters from the stable door up along the old roadway, turn homewards then, keeping by the edge of the cliff, and as he came along jump sideways over the bit of protecting wall and land on the ledge beneath, steady his mount on it as best he could or, as he said himself, go down into the boiling sea—a true saying, for even in the height of summer, if one looks down from the table of rock one sees stretches of broken foam beneath, twisting and turning or diving with agony into the black depths where the rocks go straight down.

The company left us to dress there in the loft; and silently enough we went about it, not knowing what to say to Sean for he was never an easy man to make talk with. But this is a thing we have since often spoken about among ourselves:

as we were dressing in silence, nervously, wondering if we were doing right in not stopping the whole caper, we heard the old weaver below passionately at work in the middle of the night! And it was at the selfsame moment we all found ourselves listening to his loom, and the selfsame thought must have struck into all our minds, for when Sean had finished dressing, when he had flung on his coat and blessed himself, he stood up straight and, as we all glanced at him, said with one of his strange looks: "Very well, so, very well, so," speaking quickly and quite suddenly, the very words the weaver used to say of a night-time when he rose up to the weaving. He then turned to go down.

Liam, the turf boy, had more presence of mind than the rest of us. He raced for the door and called after Sean: "'Twould be the best of your play to go and have a sconce at it," meaning the ledge. But we heard Sean descending the ladder quickly and firmly.

"What did he say?" we asked.

"Not a word," the boy answered.

For that matter, however, there was not a foot of the land that Sean did not know the look of and the feel of.

III

When we came out into the front courtyard we all stopped to note the sight before us. It was noisy and confused. Dogs and horses were everywhere. Some of the roisterers were already mounted, and others were doing their best to mount, blubbering, many of them, in a way that you'd pity. The two old coaches, one of them falling asunder, were wheeled out that the ladies might be taken to see the "midnight ride," as one of them said with a snigger. Lanterns were swinging and moving, very ruddy-looking in the cold shadows hard by the walls of the courtyard: and all was life and bustle and riding off and yelping and yowling.

Sean was in the stables choosing the horse. He pitched on

Litis, the Master's favourite mount. She was called Litis because she was a cold sort of white, without a tint of warmth
in it. Litis is an Irish word. We stood clustered about the
gates of the stables looking in at him examining her: and as
he lifted one hoof after another making sure of her shoes, we
heard him snarling through his teeth: "Very well, so, very
well, so." The ancient Brosnans, as everyone knows, were the
best horsemen in Corkaguiney. When we thought of this we
went almost cold to hear their living descendant speaking to
them in that hard and bitter way.

When he had finished he stood up and said: "Send the
Master in to me," speaking like a chieftain giving his orders.
Sir Timothy we brought to him.

" 'Tis Litis I'm riding," he said. The Master pursed out his
lips angrily, we thought, but then softened quickly; he was
afraid Sean might draw back. "Certainly. Anything you like.
I'm thankful to you." The word then went out that no one
should go nearer to the ledge than the old *lios* which looks
down over all the scene from the open hillside. It was afterwards settled, however, that the turf boy should lie in the
heather by the edge: if he kept still in that position there
was small fear that he'd frighten the hunter.

The company on their horses and the ladies in their carriages made out along the avenue for the roadway, and we
crossed the lawn and hurried through the parkland on to the
open slopes above the sea. After the darkness of the trees, the
scene was dazzling. The sun had gone down that October
evening sullenly in dusky crimson and flaming gold; afterwards the clouds cleared and a frost had fallen. The wide
stretches on the cliff tops were white with it, the silent sheep
were white with it; but wherever a streak of shadow was laid
at all it was as black as ink, and sharp and strong. The moon
was behind us, however, and only little jabs of shadow were
visible: we were looking at a sharp-edged slope of white;
beyond it was a grey mass, whether sea or sky one could not

say except when out on the reef a run of foam would catch the moon's rays for a moment, wriggle silver bright, like an eel caught in the hand, and then go out, leaving the darkness vast and vacant.

We made upwards across that white slope to the *lios;* and as we swept through the newly frozen grass and heather we left dark wet-looking tracks behind us. Far to the right we heard the gentry coming along the road. They met the herds driving the cattle to the fair in Dingle: the way was blocked by them, blocked completely, for three score cattle had been gathered together. Out raced Sir Timothy, wild with anger: "Be off with yourselves," he cried at the herds, and he ran his horse against them so viciously that they had to dive and juggle among the cattle to avoid him. "Clear the road," he bellowed, "or I'll have your lives."

They thought he had gone mad, shouting like that and leading all that rout with him along a half-forgotten road in a lonely land after the cocks had long crowed for midnight. The stock they goaded helter skelter into the bogs; and all the night afterwards we could hear the beasts crying and moaning, not knowing where they were.

We gathered to the *lios,* the gentry making their own of the raised ground within it. The Master then had all the dogs and horses taken back to the stables, fearing that some of them might make a noise or bolt off at the sound of the hoofs.

IV

"Stop that chatter," the Master cried angrily at us, and I tell you we stopped it and held our peace. A bullock, far off, began to moan.

"Do you hear that, do you hear that?" he whined in agony.

"Is Liam below?" he asked later, and someone answered: "You can see him."

"I can't," he snarled, putting an end to the talk. It was true that he could not see the boy, for we, who were younger, could hardly make out the figure on the ground, stretched out with his face almost over the edge of the cliff. If Sean did not jump, if at the last moment he took fright and raced on, 'twould go hard with the boy to save himself from the thundering hoofs.

After the lights and the yowling and the stamping of the horses and the quick, careless voices in the courtyard, the silence in which we had now to cluster together in that broken *lios* seemed to leave us without any defence against the chill in the air: we felt it settling down on our shoulders, like a cold hand; and the dainty ladies in spite of their wrappings began to shiver from head to foot.

But it was not long till we heard a lively daring galloping making up the rocky road behind us on the hill; we heard the hoofs smiting the rocky ribbings that run obliquely across that deserted roadway, and the whole wide night, as well as ourselves, seemed to listen to them as they rang out in the frosty air. Since Sir Timothy did not turn his head, we dared not do so, but even had we done so we could scarcely have seen the horseman.

Louder and louder the hoofs kept beating their rocky anvil until the crest of the hill was reached; then they softened, as if the rider was making a more careful descent.

At last we lost them; we knew then that Sean had turned in at the gap and was coming along by the cliff. It was a heavy thudding now that filled our ears. Soon we spied out what we had been peering for—a white mass bounding through the moonlit air.

That live mass suddenly seemed to burst through some veil; man and horse, at last we saw them clearly. With his long greyish stockings below his bleached corduroy knee breeches, with his white linen shirt, his fair head, he looked to be all as white as Litis herself. As they came more broadside on they shone out against the haze that covered the sea. They travelled forward with confident dash and swiftness,

and the look of them was so fine that we lifted ourselves up, forgetting our fear, forgetting the Master's commands. The pounding of the horse's hoofs was in our hearts. Our mouths were open, we heard a voice, masterful. The animal's head stretched out, threw itself up lightly. The white mass lifted itself, hung a moment in the air like a flower, then down it went, almost plumb. Not a sound then. We went cold to the marrow. The turf boy had not stirred. All our eyes were upon him. At last we saw him begin to wriggle rapidly along the edge, then to say something we could not catch—an excited voice. We strained to hear, and one of our ladies began to giggle, losing control of herself.

"Stay where ye are," whispered the Master hoarsely, and he broke from us and made down the slope. Halfway down he stopped suddenly. The turf boy had risen to his feet, was running along the edge, was crouched down again.

Then we saw Sean rise up above the top of the cliff. Quite still, erect, moon-bright, he stood with his back to the sea. From him the turf boy drew away, staring. Our Master, however, pulled himself together. He gave a wild view halloo and started to run down with his hand out towards his jockey. We all then started too to run down the slope, yet we were not certain of ourselves. For Sean stood still, erect, somehow proud, like a noble doorway awaiting a distracted mob that would find refuge within it. Breasting the full light of the moon he stood, white from head to foot, against the dull background of frosty air. His head was as high as he could hold it, and he took no notice of the Master's extended hand. So still he was he looked like a pillar stone erected in the old times on the edge of some ravine of wreckage.

We weren't surprised when the Master, drawing near, showed some confusion and unsteadiness; he even half turned to see how close to him we were. We gathered about him in kindliness. Soon we were all standing still, waiting, and then we noticed that that pillar stone of pride was trembling from head to foot. Our Master too noticed it, and in his confusion he straightway blurted out what he should have kept to himself: "Where's the animal?" The trembling lips, pale and drawn, did not speak. Our Master's confusion got still more hold of him. He was a man of no character, and in such a one the least trace of submission in another will raise heat and arrogance; he now spoke quite boldly: "I'm saying where's the animal?" Without a moment's delay he was answered:

"In the sea!"

And saying these words, the descendant of the Brosnans withdrew his eyes contemptuously from his abashed Master and strode through us all, noble and simple, as if we were so much dirt off the road.

V

It was all a bad night's work. The two great families fell out, Sir Daniel maintaining that the drowning of the animal excused him from paying the wager: and this falling out between them hastened their decay. The innocent boy who was the only witness of whatever wild thing took place between Sean and the horse on the ledge, a new look came into his eyes, into his mouth; as soon as ever he could he cleared away to America with his secret untold. And as for Sean himself—whoever knew a man that was happy and comfortable to carry his head in the air as Sean carries his?

The Stones

....

I

THOUGH John Redney's house was far back in the glen his straggling farm spread out into the river valley of which the glen itself was, as one might say, a side pocket, narrow and secret. In all its winding length there was no other house: it was even more lonely now than when long years before John Redney had played in it, a companionless child.

When the sudden downpour of rain towards the end of August swept his newly gathered cruach of turf from the inches, leaving him without fuel for the coming year, he knew quite well that all down the valley, and on the heights as well, the farmers were shaking their heads over what had befallen him, were by adding this to that, proverb to proverb, memory to memory, strengthening one another's belief that such disasters did not overtake a man without cause. And the picture he made himself of them so grouped was a pain that almost overwhelmed the pain of his actual loss.

Only two days before, he had finished the ferrying over of the turf from the bogs on the other side of the river. He had thrown it out there loosely, not far from the bank, for, the very next day, he was going to cart it up the glen to the little rise where the Redneys had built their cruach as long as anyone remembered. That very evening he had sent his labouring boy over to Con Jer for the loan of his horse and man for the next day, for the one day only to help him in drawing the turf from the inches to that traditional ground. Con Jer had answered the boy that he came at a most unfortunate time, that he had never been so busy, that he couldn't think of letting him have even the horse not to mind one of his men as well. He said he was surprised that John Redney would not have thought of that himself. Innocently enough the boy repeated the words as Con Jer had spoken them. And so it was that the next day John Redney hastened down the glen, mounted a hillock at the mouth of it, and scowled at the swirling waters rolling his turf along the valley—good black turf, as firm a sod as he had ever cut, and a whole year's supply of it, and more.

The morning after, as he gazed at the drenched fields from which the sudden mountain floods were rapidly disappearing, he could not help recalling the very words the boy had brought back in his mouth from Con Jer, nor how they had set him on fire, maddened him until he had told him angrily that it might be a good thing for Con Jer to go up to Carrigavawring and have a look at his own effigy there. No, the exact words he had used were: "Well, boy, Con Jer's effigy in stone, up there on Carrigavawring, if Con Jer went up and had a look at it—one look"—and there he had stopped. It had been in his mind to say that one glance at it would leave Con Jer with only very little thought indeed for crops or cattle or fences or anything else that concerned this world of living men. This, however, he had not said and perhaps it was better so. The boy had, he was certain, truly reported the words, only half aware of the threat in them; and repeated in that broken uncertain fashion, they had had, it might be, raised more confusion in Con Jer's mind than if they had been made into a frightful story. What did he care! Let them now come together, the farmers of the valley, stick their noses into one another's faces, make out that his turf had not been swept from him without reason—it was all one to him. Con Jer would toss and turn on his pillow for many a night to come, wondering if what the boy had reported was true and, if true, what would come of it.

More and more as he dully stared in front of him the river was reassuming its own true shape. Through the levels of the valley it curved from side to side with the light of the day, although it was a grey day, thick upon its surface, causing the pasture lands on either side to look dark and heavy. If the Nyhans had flung up a bit of a dam where the engineer had told them, there was an end to those sudden floodings; but no, the Nyhans hadn't it in them even to help themselves, when by doing so they would help another. The whole lot of them, the farmers on this side and the other, were against him.

II

It is a stony land. The name of it, Kilclaw, might mean either the Stone Church or the Stony Wood. Nobody now knows which. The woods were felled some hundreds of years ago; but felling the trees had not been sufficient, for, that done, even the roughest kind of tillage was not yet possible until the little patches first marked out for it had been cleared of the largest of the stones embedded in them. The roots of them were found to be tougher than those of the wild ash, the mountain fir, or the oak. Yet removed they were, dragged to the sides of the little fields, however they managed it, crop upon crop of them, year after year, decade after decade, century after century, until the stone mounds that now enclose the little patches of wheat or oats or potatoes take up as much, if not more, of the ground than the croppings within them. The boulders earliest removed were huge, huger than would now appear, for their bases once again are hidden deep in the ground. Halfway up their flanks, sometimes all the way, they are clothed with brown and silvery mosses, or with innumerable layers of the tiniest fern.

On top of and around and between them thousands and thousands of smaller stones have been piled or flung; and these, more exposed to the winds and rain and sunshine, have not clothed themselves at all, remain still unclad, may remain forever unclad, unsoftened with verdure, bleached-looking, bare and stark. The people of the place fancy they see in them—those moss-clad boulders, those skull-like smaller stones that surmount them, effigies, images of their neighbours, never of themselves. A farmer using the *poirse* of a neighbour as a short cut for his turf or corn may suddenly behold, in some place that he has already passed by some hundreds of times, the rough effigy of one of the dwellers in the valley. If however, he be wise and of good heart he will keep his discovery to himself, for it bodes no one any good, this unexpected revelation of one's image in the stones.

John Redney never had been either wise or of good heart. His mind dwelt too much on things that were abroad in the air, in the darkness, drifting hither and thither. He was a poor lonely creature, living there in that unvisited glen, his the only house within it. His children were scattered far from him, were not writing to him, it was said, and his wife had become long since a poor sorry drudge to him. Having loosed that word effigy upon the wind, he went uselessly and restlessly strealing about his straggling fields more silent and gloomy than ever. He came to know that Con Jer had laughed at the threat, had said, "And John Redney wants me to mount up to Carrigavawring and have a look at myself! I won't then. I have something else to do." But Redney knew that if that laughter of Con Jer's was loud it was also hollow. He felt quite certain that Con Jer did not laugh in his heart when he laid his head on the pillow in the darkness.

III

At this time arrived one who had long since outgrown the beliefs of the hillsides—the ex-soldier, Jack Lambert, Miles

Lambert's good-for-nothing son. He had slaved and tramped his way in England, had been in America, Canada, and Australia—and nowhere had done any good. He had found himself in the Great War, first in France, then in Gallipoli. Again and again he had come back to his father's house and again wandered off from it whither he would. He had been at home this time only a week or so when the news was abroad that he had been seen in Redney's company traversing the most hidden and ill-reputed places at unearthly hours. Even on nights that were stormy and wild and without a glimpse of either moonlight or starlight, the two of them were heard going by. On quieter nights the sounds of the footsteps of the two of them had wakened people from their sleep, had caused them to lift their heads to listen. Johneen Kelleher had been out in his fields before the dawn drawing the stooks together, making them ready for the help that was to come to him as soon as the sun had dried the corn—and those two misguided men he had seen coming down from the stony hills where there were neither houses nor tilled fields nor traffic, and they looked as if they had been abroad the livelong night! Over his story a dozen heads drew into a circle; and one and then another remarked how much Lambert was changing; how he had taken on strange airs, had been found staring intently into this man's haggard, and elsewhere, in a place where he could have had no business, had suddenly raised his head above a mound of stones. Besides they had all noticed how, whenever he chanced to meet them now upon the road, he would look through them as if he knew the very thoughts they were thinking. Yet it was not he they blamed. He they knew was but the empty book into which old Redney was writing all the perversity he had ever indulged in that crabbed brain of his. Larry Condon broke up their discussion with a free gesture. What was Lambert but a common bummer, sponging on Redney, who, fool that he was, God knows he was queer since the day he was born, had

been glad to find anyone at all to strike up a friendship with,
to drink with, to gossip with; and none of them could deny
that Lambert was a man of fine discourse when he had swallowed down a glass or two of good whiskey. They all knew
as well as he did that Lambert gave no credence to those
beliefs of theirs. Since they had often defended their beliefs
against him this they could not argue against, whereupon,
silenced for the time, they broke the gathering and went
through the darkness each to his lonely house. But by the
next night some other tidings of the two secret men would
have floated into some farmyard or other and another discussion would take place around the hearth. The faces of
the two of them, the look of intentness in them, began now
to abide in the memory of all who crossed them. Whatever
had come to possess them! the people asked one another.
Were the two of them determined not to cease their searching until they had discovered the effigies of all the farmers
of Kilclaw? Fear spread from house to house along the valley.
There was not now a dweller in it who, if he spied the two of
them coming towards him along the road, would not turn
aside into some farmer's *poirse* to escape the peering of their
eyes.

IV

They were an ill-matched pair: Lambert, the ex-soldier,
brazen-eyed, straight-lipped, withered-skinned, impudent,
and with a reckless way of striding along: old Redney, shy
and tongue-tied, looking out from under his shaggy brows,
his head down, his left hand clenched across the small of
his back, his right hand tight and heavy upon the knob of his
stick. With quick, uncertain steps, he made forwards as if
his secret knowledge was no happy cargo. The neighbours
would see him hobbling along with Lambert, always a little
in the rear. They would see him stop up, his stick directed
across a valley or along the flank of a mountain while Lam-

bert's eyes searched the distance indicated; or Lambert they would find looking back over his shoulder waiting for the other as he clambered clumsily over those fences of loose stones. And the same anxiety arose again and again:

"Are they burying the whole countryside of us?"

"And what will they gain by it?"

"Nothing except the pacifying of their own wicked minds."

" 'Tis a frightful thing for a man to know that he is already in the stone, that he is there to be seen for all time. If you woke up in the dead of the night, a wild night or a night of hard frost, you wouldn't like to picture it. You'd feel the frost in your shoulder bones."

But those who gathered of a night time to Con Jer's were a quiet lot; Lambert and Redney might by dint of searching come on the images of the whole countryside and they would not lift an arm to prevent it. The younger men who met after the day in Dan Owen's were different. It was Pat Early, whose shoulder blow would fell a bullock, determined for that group what they should do.

The next day they loitered around the tumbledown cabin where their one smith kept his forge. Into its smoky background they retired, all of them except Pat Early himself, when they discovered that Lambert was coming along the road. From within they heard the approaching footsteps: they then heard Pat Early's voice: "Lambert," he said, with a rasping tone, "Come over here."

They heard the footsteps cease. Pat's voice they heard again:

"Come over here. I have a word to say to you."

They could now see Lambert in the brightness of the doorway, his back almost towards them:

"Well?" he said.

"Did you hear Pat Nyhan is after dying on them?"

"I didn't: where would I hear it?"

Though he answered glibly enough, those within thought

they saw him start when Pat flung the unexpected question at him.

"If you knew he was going to meet his end, sudden, and without preparation, you might have warned him: 'twould be a neighbourly act."

They expected Lambert to deny, if only for safety's sake, any foreknowledge of Pat Nyhan's death; but the words they heard were:

"Is this a place for neighbourly acts?"

His next word then they felt would be either of old Redney's cruach of turf that the August flood had swept down the valley or else of the Nyhans' failure to build the rampart which would forever save the levels from the swollen river. Pat Early, however, gave him no time: he blazed out:

"Why don't you answer the question I put to you?"

"Question!"

"Did you know—did you know that something was in store for Pat Nyhan, some misfortune or other?"

"Two nights ago," he answered after a slight pause and quite in a low voice, "John Redney showed me him in the stone."

They grew cold to hear him. And he had said the words in a way that showed that himself was no longer a mocker. Pat Early cried out quickly and with great strength and warmth, to their great relief:

" 'Tis a lie!"

Lambert, however, who had turned to go, was not disturbed either by the words or the force in them; he looked back and said in the same low voice:

"If he showed—the sight to me he can show it to you, that is if you care to see it, now the man's dead. Some people mightn't like to."

The listeners gathered out noiselessly from the shelter of the forge, all of them; they feared that Pat Early was shaken, but again sturdily he answered:

"See what? A couple of stones! Do you think I believe old Redney has power over us?"

"But you'd face it?"

"I'd face a couple of stones anyhow."

"We'd all do that," John Morian added.

"By day or night?"

" 'Tis equal."

"Very well; I'll tell himself."

V

It was now the end of November. The night, it seemed, could not hold any more stars, nor the air any more cold. Con Jer's son, Tadhg, was one of the whispering group. Others were Pat Early, his brother-in-law, Michael Glynn, the smith's son, Larry Mehigan, and the teacher's son, Jim Carey, who had ventured without his father's knowledge. Morian was with them also. Larry Mehigan was delicate: the piercing cold had urged to rapid walking, and they had mounted Knockanuller at one spurt before they were suddenly aware of his gasping, of his effort to keep up with them:

"Are we going too fast?" Michael Glynn said.

"I'll be all right in a minute," Larry answered; but immediately he had to turn aside doubled up in a fit of coughing.

" 'Twas the cold made us hurry: 'twas a queer thing for us to do."

"But 'tisn't good to be stopping here; that's the devil of a wind for him."

"There's shelter beyond."

" 'Tis more than twenty years since I was up in these places."

"Who'd come up here? What business would you have?"

"We'll be going on now."

"How far up he came to find poor Pat Nyhan's image."

They thought of him rigid in his bed.

" 'Tis a frightful night to be dead on."

They did not laugh. Another time they would have done so at such awkward words, but dimly in the starlight they individually spied out shoulders of whitish rock and boulders that looked like massive ancient, long-weathered skulls. The little narrow path they were on was bordered by some of those immemorial pilings of stones, large and small. The mounds kept the wind from them, but the open spaces of the bogland would have been more welcome to them. "Look, they're waiting for us."

Sitting in the shelter of an upright slab of rock they saw the two figures; Redney's rigid grasp of the knob of his stick they noticed especially.

"Are ye waiting long?" Pat Early said, casually, he hoped.

"Mind ye," old Redney answered, " 'tisn't by my wish ye're up here at all; far from it."

Pat Early thought he wished to put them off. "If you can show us what Lambert said, 'tis right you should."

"I can show ye that all right, since ye wish it."

They all began to move forward. In the dim light the round water-worn stones in the *poirse* began to roll under their feet. Pat Early said:

"I see we would have done right to have our spectacles with us to see it."

Only after a few moments the old man understood the words. He then said, calmly and coldly:

"There'll be light enough where 'tis. The moon's there already."

As he spoke he raised his stick towards the brow of the hill, which was gapped and rugged with boulders and rocks. There the sky was becoming more and more luminous and the stars were gone. The moon they understood to be away towards the right. When they pierced through among the boulders they saw it suddenly, rising in splendour. Slabs of blanched stone, pillar stones of shadow, gaps of darkness—

sharp-edged, were all about them in confusion. They felt astray.

"There's Pat Nyhan. The Nyhans were up here always."

Even if, with his stick, he had not pointed out the particular group of stones in that long-deserted mountain farm ground they would have known it for Pat Nyhan. It was set up in a listening attitude, Pat Nyhan's attitude; just so he used to listen, his left ear advanced, for he had been for years a little hard of hearing. They recollected too having heard that the Nyhans had come from this place. As they looked they could swear they saw the stones stir. One or two of the men fidgeted, looking around. Others stared at the stones in a dull sort of way. They were conscious of a desire to strike old Redney or the ex-soldier, yet conscious also that that was not in the bargain. The ex-soldier stood a little apart from them, neither looking nor speaking. Suddenly Larry Mehigan with that burred and resonant consumptive's voice of his said:

"Up here too the Redneys were always. I heard tell of them."

Their eyes swept from the image and fastened on Redney. He turned his back on them as if he would set off for home. Indistinctly he grumbled at them over his shoulder:

"Ye're after seeing what ye came to see."

He put out his left hand and Lambert came and folded it in his arm, protectingly. They then began to move off, the two of them. The others hesitated. As soon as he had said the words, Mehigan had been taken with a fit of coughing. The stone desert was ringing with the sound of it, and the dogs in distant farmyards had awakened and were answering back. But the dogs' barking Larry heard no more than he heard his own coughing: his excited brain was working all the time; he would blurt out, not giving the spasm time to exhaust itself:

" 'Tis true what I say. Up here they were always, the Red-neys."

"Somehow that's true. I heard it said; 'twas said," Morian gave his opinion earnestly.

They came closer together. They were thankful to Larry. His words excused them from looking around any more at the stone image, listening in the way that a tall deaf old man would listen.

Larry's cough had ceased, and they began to hasten after the two others. When they got within a short distance of them they saw old Redney stop up rather suddenly and rais-ing his stick, point out something to Lambert. A word how-ever he did not speak. The whole of them stopped up where they were. Individually fright fell on them. They did not want to know what the old man was pointing at. Lambert seemed vexed and impatient. They heard his whisper: "Come on, come on." But old Redney seemed not to be able to move nor to change his attitude. The moon poured its light on them all: old Redney with his stick stretched out, Lambert a little apart from him, waiting impatiently, and the other group still farther apart, puzzled and anxious. The cold was intense, and the sparkling earth was as silent as the starry heavens. The distant farm dogs had put their noses again upon the ground. It was their own stillness made the men aware of the benumbed stillness about them.

"Come on, come on," they again heard whispered very hoarsely, and Lambert made a stride towards the petrified figure of his friend. As he neared it they saw the stick fall clattering to the frozen ground, and the next moment they saw Redney fling himself helplessly into Lambert's arms, a thin whimpering wail breaking from him into the silence.

"Look!" the boy Jim Carey cried; and right beyond the two clutching figures they saw old Redney in stone! The image was dark against the sky and immensely larger than the poor stricken thing in the ex-soldier's arms. It seemed

to mock him, the head of it stretched out in unrelenting eagerness. One glance they gave it and without a word broke
from the place.

Jack Lambert a few days afterwards was seen driving from
the place, no one knew whither. Old Redney was missed.
His poor bedraggled wife they would see driving the cows
of a night time to the inches. She kept her thoughts to herself.
Only after weeks and weeks the men of the valley learned
her husband had taken to his bed, awaiting his doom. In
tongue-tied silence still he awaits it, his eyes staring out
straight before him.

The Awakening

....

I

IVOR O'DONOVAN knew it was Ted Driscoll had called him: raising himself above the edge of the bunk he was just in time to see him manœuvring that bear-like body of his through the narrow little hatchway, to see the splintery shutter slap to behind him. At the same moment he heard the Captain clearing his throat. The bunk opposite was his, and now Ivor saw him, all limbs, mounting awkwardly yet carefully over the edge of it. What between the sprawling limbs, the ungainly body and the hovering shadows above them, the place was narrowed to the size of a packing case. The timber work of the cabin had become so dark with the smoke of the stove that neither shadows nor limbs seemed to stir except when their movements were sudden and jerky. Ivor soon heard the Captain gathering his oil-cloths from the floor with one hand while with the other he dragged at the bunk where the cabin boy was sleeping; this Ivor knew, for as he sat up he caught the familiar words:

"Come on, come on; rouse up; they'll be waiting."

The Captain he then saw disappear through the toy-like hatchway.

Ivor O'Donovan himself with a stifled groan descended lifelessly from the bunk to the floor. He drew on his sea boots —they had been his father's—drew his oil-cloths about him and in turn thrust his hand into the warm pile of old coats and sacking in which the sleeping boy was buried. He shook him vigorously: "Come on, come on; they'll be waiting," he said, and then hurried aloft into the drizzling darkness and took his place with the others.

The tightness that he felt on his brain from the moment Ted Driscoll had roused him seemed natural, not unexpected; nevertheless he groaned to recollect the cause of it. Now, however, as he settled down to his night's work, planted in the darkness there at the gunwale, braced against it, facing the Captain, the dripping fish-laden incoming net between them, he noticed that the tightness had somehow slackened, was still loosening its grip of him, so much so that he had some fear that it would again suddenly pounce on him with its first heat and violence.

Ted Driscoll and Tom Mescall were forward at the windlass; beyond them the boy, bending down, was coiling the rope they passed to him.

It was very dark. Everything was huge and shapeless. Anchored as she was, tethered besides, clumsy with the weight of dripping fish-spangled net coming in over the gunwale, the nobby was tossed and slapped about with a violence that surprised him; flakes of wet brightness were being flung everywhere from the one lamp bound firmly to the mast. Yet the night was almost windless, the sea apparently sluggish: there must be, he thought, a stiff swell beneath them. What most surprised him, however, was to find himself thinking about it. That evening coming down the harbour, he would not have noticed it. The whole way out, his back to the sea, he had stood upright, his feet set wide apart, his hands in his belt, glum, silent, gazing at the cabin boy who, sprawled upon the deck, was intent upon the baited line he had flung over the stern. But as far as Ivor was concerned that patch of deck might have been free to the sun: his own anger, his passion, was between him and the world. That afternoon he had waited for Chrissie Collins for two hours. At the very start he knew, he *knew,* so at least he had told himself she would not come. For all that he had gone hot and cold, again and again, while waiting for her. He had broken from the spot impulsively: a moment later he had trailed back again, giving her one more quarter of an hour to make good in. Then when his rage was at the peak, hurrying down to the jetty, he had suddenly caught sight of her, all brightness, stepping briskly up the hillside, the schoolmaster walking beside her, as eager as herself. Her head was bent, her eyes were fixed on her dainty toe-caps, and she was listening complacently to the schoolmaster's blather. Only that he should have to tear through the village and it filled with the gathering crews, he'd have told her what he thought of her.

With his eyes downwards on the sprawling limbs of the boy, he had indulged, as if it were the only thing for a man to do, the heat of the passion that that one glimpse of her had aroused in him.

Now, ten hours later, braced against the timbers, swaying and balancing, freeing the net, freeing the rope, grabbing at the odd dog fish, the odd blob of seaweed, the tangle of seawrack, flinging them all, as they came, far out, clear of the rising meshes—he was puzzled to contrast his present indifference with his stifling anger of the afternoon. Yet he was not pleased with himself. This calming down of his seemed like a loss of manhood. His mind could not, it appeared, stay fixed on the one thought. He found himself noticing what he had never noticed before—how the mackerel, entangled in the meshes, would catch the light of the worried lamp and appear just like a flight of shining steel-bright daggers hurtling by him from gunwale to hold. Never to have noticed so striking a thing before, how curious! But had the Captain ever noticed it? He glanced shyly at the aged face opposite him and started, for the Captain, he saw, had had his eyes fixed on him, all the time, perhaps! And Ivor recalled, reddening slightly, that also that afternoon while lost in his own passionate thoughts he had caught him observing him with the selfsame silent gravity. Why should he do it? He was Captain. But the boat was his, Ivor's; and one day when he was somewhat older, and when his mother was willing to trust him, he would sail it. But this was unfair, he felt, for the Captain, this Larry Keohane, had been ever and always his father's dearest friend and shipmate, had sailed with him till he was drowned, had indeed been with him that very night; and afterwards he it was who had undertaken the management of the boat for them; and in such a way that not a penny of the fish money had ever gone astray on them. Later on, now two years ago, he had taken Ivor on board as one of the crew, and taught him whatever he now knew of sailoring and deep sea fishing. There was surely plenty of time yet for thinking of playing the Captain. Besides, the selling of the fish was trickier work than the catching of it. His eyes fell on the claw-like hands of the Captain, they were twisted with rheumatism, and a flood of kindly feeling for this grave and faithful friend suddenly swept over him with such power that he found his own hands fumbling at the net without either skill or strength in them. To glance again at the Captain's face he did not dare.

"Up, boys, up!" he impulsively cried to the windlass men as if to encourage them. In the clinging darkness, although the drizzle was becoming lighter and lighter, he could make out only the shapeless bulk of themselves and the windlass: two awkward lumps of manhood rising and falling alternately, their sou'westers and oil-cloths catching some of the flakes of the wet brightness that were flying around everywhere. 'Twas curious work, this fishing. Like a family they were, confined in a tiny space, as far almost from the other boats as they were from the houses on the hills where the real families were now huddled together in sleep. The real families—each of them was different from the others. Tom Mescall's was the most good-for-nothing in the whole place.

Others had quite nice houses, clean and well-kept. But most strange of all was it to have him, Ivor, thinking of such things, his head calm and cool (and he thereupon grabbed a huge dog-fish from the passing net and with a gesture deliberately sweeping sent it far out into the splashing darkness).

II

The work went on and on and Ivor could not help all kinds of thoughts from crossing his brain, nor help noticing the onward rush of them. The dragging of the net was done in silence, no one speaking until they each and all were sure that they had had a fairly good catch, and that all the nets were heavy. Ivor then was aware that some dull and lifeless conversation was passing to and fro between the men at the windlass. He was hailed suddenly by one of them, Ted Driscoll: "Look where Leary is, east."

Far off, east, Ivor saw a tiny light. As he watched it the other voice came through the darkness, half speaking, half calling:

"'aith then he wouldn't be long swinging on to the Galley in there."

"Is it Leary, do you think?" Ivor asked the Captain, and he was answered:

"'Tis like the place he'd be."

Ivor then sent his gaze ranging the sea noting the disposition of the boats. They were far off, nearly all of them. Some were miles beyond Galley Head. Others were away towards the west. Here and there a pair of lights seemed to ride close together, only seemed, however, while an odd one, like Leary's, played the hermit in unaccustomed waters. Far to the west the great light of the Fastnet every few moments threw a startling beam on the waters and, quenching suddenly, would leave a huge blackness suspended before their very eyes, blinding them. He noticed how, little by little, the

timid lamps of the fishing fleet would in time manage again
to glimmer through that darkness. He bent himself once more
on the work, thinking over and over again what a curious way
they had of making a living. On the land at this time of night
every one of the houses was a nest of sleep—chilly walls
and warm bedding. After all Chrissie Collins was a farmer's
daughter, a small hillside farmer, a "sky" farmer. Farm houses
had ways of their own. Fishermen also had ways of their own.
The next time he met her he would hold his head as high as
hers.

The dragging went on and on. The unending clanking of
the windlass, the wet mass of the net, the grip of his feet on
the narrow way between gunwale and hold while the boat
tossed and tugged, the sudden flashes of the lamp, the long
silences of them all, the far-off lonely looking lights of the
other anchored nobbies and ketches, the bold startling blaze
of the Fastnet, and above all the stream of shining daggers
sweeping by—for the first time in his life he reckoned up the
features of the fisherman's calling, and felt some sort of
pleasant excitement in doing so, as if he had heard some good
news or come upon some unexpected treasure. He could not
understand it.

When the last of the nets was in they tidied the decks,
pitching the seawrack into the sea. He heard the Captain
say to Driscoll, whose head was bent down on the confused
mass of fish and net in the hold: "Good, and a fair size too.
I'm very glad."

"I'm very glad," repeated Ivor in his mind, wonderingly,
yet feeling that the words fitted in. He noticed Driscoll and
Mescall, their arms hanging heavily after their night's work,
their sea boots lumping noisily along the deck, going aft to
the little cabin, making down the hatchway without a word.
The boy had gone down previously. The waft of the smell
of boiling fish, of boiling potatoes, that came from the smoke
pipe told of his toil below. To Ivor it was very welcome. He

was hungry; and besides they would presently all meet together round the little stove, "I'm very glad," he whispered,
not knowing why. And the smoke, he saw, was like a lighted
plume rising from the top of the iron pipe.

The Captain drew closer to him. He took the fragment of
pipe from his mouth and, smothering the glowing bowl in his
fist, pointed sou'west:

" 'Tis Casey that's going in."

"Is it?" Ivor said, also picking out the one craft in all
the far-scattered fleet that had got under weigh that—very
slowly, for there was scarcely a breath of wind—was making
for the land.

"Maybe 'tisn't," the Captain then said.

"I'm sure 'tis him all right," Ivor said, though he was not
sure at all.

They stood side by side following with their eyes the distant slow-moving light. There was scarcely a morning that
some boat or other did not hoist sail the moment their catch
was made and hasten in. There was always some special reason for it. And the other craft, every one of them, would make
guesses at the boat, as also at the cause of her lifting anchor
in such haste. The others were content to make the pier any
time before the buyers had received from other fishing ports
and from Dublin itself their morning telegrams fixing the
day's prices. Ivor thought how it was nearly always something having to do with the real household, with the real
family, that brought a fisherman to break that way from the
fishing grounds before the others. Sickness, or the necessity
for some early journey, or the emigrating of a son or daughter.
"I remember your father, one time we were out, and far out
too, south the Galley, ten mile it might be, how he called out
and we not ready at all: 'That'll do, boys, we'll make in.'"

The Captain's quiet husky voice stopped, and Ivor wondered if that was all he had to say; but the tale was taken up
again:

"That was twenty-two years ago this month."

Ivor was once more astray, he could not find reason in the words.

"Yes," he said, quietly.

"That night he expected a son to be born to him; and he wasn't disappointed."

Ivor knew that he himself was the child that on that night came into the world; but what kept him silent was the Captain's gravity. Such matter among them had always been a cause for laughter. Ivor was nevertheless glad that the Captain had spoken seriously; for all that, fearing to betray his own state of mind, he answered:

"That's not what's taking Casey in anyhow."

The Captain did not seem to hear.

"All night long," he said, "I'm thinking of things that I saw happen out here on these waters for the last fifty-four years."

Ivor raised his head in astonishment. Why should such recollections have set the Captain examining him the whole night long?

"Strange things," the Captain resumed, "strange voices, sad things too, very sad, things that should not happen."

After all, the Captain was in the humour for spinning a yarn, that was all. But, instead of the yarn, the Captain, scanning the sky, merely said:

" 'Tis going south; the day will be fine, very fine."

Ivor too felt a slight stir in the air, and from the hatchway Driscoll called them down.

"With God's help 'twill be a fine day," the Captain said once more, throwing the words over his shoulder as they moved aft, one behind the other, sauntering along in their heavy sea boots.

III

The air in the cabin was reeking with the smell of fish and potatoes, and so thick with fire smoke and tobacco smoke that one could hardly make things out. There was hardly room for the five of them there. The boxes they sat on were very low and the men's knees, on which they held the plates, seemed to fill the whole space. One felt the warmth against one's face like a cushion. Yet Ivor welcomed it all—the heat, the smell of the good food, the close companionship—not alone for the comfort it all wrapped him round with but for the memory it raised in him of those many other nights on which he had experienced it, his body as cold as ice and his fingers unable to move themselves. The others were already eating lustily and noisily.

"Not too bad, not too bad," he cried out cheerily, planting himself between Driscoll and Mescall, just because they were head to head and nose to nose in earnest argument. They took no notice of him, continuing it still across his very face. Driscoll, who was the simplest of them, was showing how Mrs. O'Connor, the shopkeeper who supplied them with all and sundry, had done him out of two and elevenpence, and Mescall, who, in spite of his harum-scarum wife and family, was their merrymaker, was explaining how she had tried the same trick with him and how he had laid a trap for her and caught her—a trap so clever that Driscoll had no idea how it worked or how by using it he could recover his two and elevenpence. The boy was heard plunging vessels in a bucket of water. All the time the Captain held his peace, and Ivor, noticing it, glanced at him, wondering if he were still recalling what he had seen happen on the fishing grounds during his long lifetime upon them.

Leisurely yet ravenously the meal went on, and when they thought of it, or at least so it seemed, first Mescall and then Driscoll, who had had no sleep till then, threw off their sea boots and disappeared into the darkness of the bunks. In the same haphazard way Ivor, the Captain, and the boy returned to the deck.

IV

At last they had her moving: her sails were flapping, coming suddenly between their eyes and the dazzling flood of light outwelling from sea and sky. When they filled, when she settled down, Ivor heard the Captain say in a voice that sounded unusual:

"I suppose I may as well go aft."

Unable to account for the words Ivor answered in mere confusion of mind:

" 'Tis better, I suppose," as if the matter was not quite clear.

Silently the Captain went aft to the tiller, and Ivor, as was his custom, threw himself on the pile of rope in the bow: there was no more to be done. He felt the streaming sun, into which a benign warmth was beginning to steal, bathing his body from his hair down. After the work of the night, after the food, a pleasant lassitude, as thick as his thick clothing, clung to him. The cabin boy was already fast asleep on the deck, cuddled up like a dog, his face buried in his arms. Ivor felt sleepy too, yet before he yielded to it, he recalled the memory of the handful of them, cut off from all other company, working silently in the drizzling darkness, the tossing lamp momentarily flashing in their eyes and lighting up their dripping hands. He recollected too the rise and fall of the awkward bodies of the two men at the windlass, the clanking of the axle, and the uncompanioned boy beyond them working away in almost total darkness. Clearer than all he recalled the flight of glittering spear heads sweeping by between himself and the Captain. Then also the group in the smoky cabin, the hearty faces, the blue and white plates, the boy plunging the vessels in the water. How different from what was now before his eyes! The sea was wide, wide; the air brisk, the seagulls screaming, quarrelling, gathering in schools, dashing at the transparent crests of the waves or sweeping in great curves to the east, the west, everywhere, their high-pitched cries filling the air with a rapture that opened the heart and at the same time alarmed it. Yes, very different, yet his pictures of the night time—the groups silently working in the darkness, the gathering in the little cabin—these were dearer to him just now than the bright freshness of the morning. He recalled the unexpected words of the Captain—"I'm very glad."

At last the drowsiness that he would keep from him overpowered him.

He awoke to find the boy's hand timidly unclutching his shoulder:

"Himself wants you."

Rising up he caught the Captain's eyes resting upon him with a calmness that surprised him, that disturbed him. He went aft.

"You're wanting me?"

"Sit down there, Ivor, there's a thing I have to say to you."

Fearing some reference to Chrissie Collins, some questioning, some good advice, Ivor sat down without a word. The Captain blurted out:

"Ivor, boy, 'tis time for you to sail what belongs to you."

As he spoke his hand lifted from the tiller—an instinctive giving up of office. Instantly however it fell upon it again. Ivor perceived the action with his eyes, not with his mind, for the words had sent a thrill of delight through his whole body. Everything he had been noticing that night of nights was in that overwhelming sensation—the darkness, the clanking windlass, the shining fish, the cabin, the seagulls, everything—but he caught hold of himself and said:

"But, Lar, why that? Why that?"

"Because 'tis time for you."

"But why so? 'Tisn't how you're going from us; what's after happening?"

"Nothing. Nothing. Only all the night I'm thinking of it. 'Tis the right thing. Herself is at me too. If there's a touch of wind in the night, she don't sleep a wink."

"Oh! If the boat goes we all go."

"You can't talk to them like that. Anyway 'tis right. 'Tis your due. We got on well, Ivor. Them that's gone, they deserved as much. We done our best, all of us."

"Lar, 'tis better wait till my mother hears of it."

"If you wouldn't mind I'd give you Pat to be in my place. He'd be better for you than a stranger."

Again that thrill of delight went through him. He thought at once if the Captain had not offered his son, a stranger would have to be brought into the boat, one of those unlucky creatures perhaps who had given the best of their lives sailoring the wide world over, creatures who were not trustworthy, who had bitter, reckless tongues, who destroyed the spirit of goodwill in any boat they ever got footing in. That danger the Captain had put aside. There was therefore a clear way before him, and a boat's crew after his own heart.

"I'm thankful, Lar, and herself will be thankful; but what will you be doing with yourself?"

A little smile grew upon the Captain's face, and both of them raised their eyes to scan the hillsides they were approaching. In the sun which now lay thick upon their brown-green flanks, nestling in the zig-zag ravines they saw the little groups of houses where the fishermen lived. Some of the cottages, snow-white, faced full in the eyes of the morning, sunning themselves. Others were turned aside, still asleep in the shadows, catching a bright ray only on chimney head or gable.

"Wouldn't I want to sit in the sun and smoke my pipe as well as another? That will do, Ivor. Ted's coming up. He's after smelling the land. In the evening I'll fix up with your mother."

V

It was a Saturday morning. That night and the next they would all sleep in their own houses, not in the boats.

In the evening the Captain went to Ivor's house, and, as he said himself, fixed things up with his mother. Then he shook hands with them all, with Mrs. O'Donovan, Ivor, his two sisters, and his young brother, who was only a boy. He then set off up the hill for his home.

Afterwards, standing up before the bit of glass nailed against the wall, Ivor stood shaving himself. His heart was blazing within him, his cheeks burning, for the Captain had been speaking his praises, and all his people had been staring at him.

It had been a day of uninterrupted sunshine, and now a bright heaven, slow to darken itself, although the sun had been a long time sunken, darkened to blackness every ridge, bush, tree clump, roof and gable that stood against it. On the roads and fields it still threw down a persistent glow; and Ivor went in and out the doorway praying for the dusk to thicken. In the midst of the Captain's praise of him he had felt a burning desire to see his boat once again with his own eyes, to be sure it was still there at the pier, where, with scores of others, it was fastened. He wanted to feel the tiller beneath his right hand—that above all. And yet he would not care to have any of his neighbours see him doing so. Nightfall was never so slow in coming. At last, however, with a yearning look at the still livid sky he set off down the path towards the roadway. He could gambol, he could sing, only that at the same time he had thoughts of the heavy responsibility that in future would rest upon him. He strove to calm himself, to walk with the appearance of one who had no other business than to breathe the cool air of the evening. He knew there would be groups of men still in the public-houses as well as along the sea wall; and these he wished to escape.

Before entering the village he vaulted over the wall, descended the rocks, and made along by the edge of the waters. At a point beyond the farthest house he climbed on to the road again, and, more assured, made towards the deserted pier. At its extreme end, almost, his *Wildwood* was moored. The pier itself, the debris on it, the fish boxes, the ranks of barrels—as well as all the conglomeration of boats along its sheltered side—the whole had become one black mass sharply cut out against the livid waters of the harbour. On a standard at its very end a solitary oil lamp, as warm in colour as the waters were cold, was burning away in loneliness. Towards it, and as quietly, almost as stealthily as if on a guilty errand, he steered his way. He was glad when the piles of barrels so obstructed the view that no one could spy him from the road. Doubtless the news was already abroad; by now the men were surely all speaking about it; as for himself, it was very strange coming at the time it did, coming, without expectation, at the tail-end of the night when for the first time he knew what it was to be a true fisherman. He was glad Chrissie Collins had her schoolmaster. It left himself as free as air. And thinking the thought he breathed in the pleasant coolness of the night, yet could not, it seemed, gulp down enough of it. Glad of the darkness, of the loneliness, he suddenly threw out his two arms wide apart, stretching them from him, and drew the keen air slowly and deliciously through his nostrils. And breathing still in the self-same manner went forward a few steps. Then suddenly, he saw a figure, outlined against the tide, seated on some fish boxes, gazing silently at the nobby for which he himself was making! He knew it was the Captain. His arms fell and he stood quite still.

"Oh!" he said, in a sudden stoppage of thought. He turned stealthily and retraced his steps, fearful of hearing his name cried out. But nothing was to be heard except his own careful footfall; and before he reached the road again he had re-

covered himself. It surely was a sad thing for Larry Keohane
to have his life drawing to an end. Why was it that nothing
can happen to fill one person with happiness without bringing sadness and pain to somebody else? Yet the Captain, he
remembered, that evening in his mother's house had been
quite cheerful, had told them how glad he was that they
had made quite a good catch on his last night, and what a
peaceful night it had been! And what a fine boat the *Wildwood* was; and how happy he was to be leaving her in hands
that would not treat her foully; indeed he could well say that
he was flinging all responsibility from his shoulders; and that
was a thing he had been looking forward to for a long time.
And saying that, he had gone from them cheerily and
brightly. Yes, yes, but here surely was the real captain, this
seaman staring at his boat.

Ivor waited, sitting on the wall in the darkness, for a long
time. At last he heard the slow steps of the old man approaching, saw him pass by—saw him very indistinctly for
the darkness, yet knew that he had his hand covering his
pipe in his mouth and his head on one side, a way he had
when he was thinking to himself. He waited until the footsteps had died away up the hillside; then he rose to resume
his own quest towards the nobby. He found he could not
bring himself to do so. He did not want to do so.

With slow lingering steps, with stoppings and turnings,
at last he too began to make towards his home. His head was
flung up, almost flung back. More than once he told himself that he didn't ever remember the sky to have been so full
of stars. Somehow he felt like raising his hand towards them.

The Emptied Sack

I

URGED to it by his son, John Connole made up his mind to do as the other potters had done; to throw aside the ancient methods, the antique gear he had inherited from his fathers, as they from theirs, and to install—it was his son's word—to install instead a modern scientific furnace in which the heat could be regulated to the hundredth part of a degree. Old Tadhg Kinnane, that dwarf-like creature, stooped and venomous, more than eighty years of age, whose body some intensity of brain rather than warmth of heart kept alive—what would *he* do then? With his heaped-up donkey-load of furze branches piled higher than his head he would no more be seen in the streets of Youghal, for furze was not the tinder used in the new-fashioned furnaces.

"And the poor creature," Jack Tattan, one of the potters, began, half smiling, his hands under his clay-white apron, "'tis little use he's now for anything else."

"He's eighty, he must be eighty-three," Fred Lincoln said, his eyes twinkling against the sun; he had just come from within.

"Why should he be working at all? What is he working for? All he earned his whole life long, what did he do with it?"

"'Twill be worse for him than the *Calliope*."

"It will that."

Forty years ago when the *Calliope* lay along the jetties all

50

the windows of the hillside town gazed wide-eyed at her
bright shapeliness. Her gilded points and lines, her whiteness, her sparkle, her shining newness, had bespoken welcome for her from the townsfolk; her crew, from captain to
cabin boy, were given the run of the port. Tadhg Kinnane
was then in the prime of life, forty years of age, yet had for
all that already buried his household—parents, wife, children, all except one daughter—had buried them in Ardmore of the Saints across the water. That daughter he had
taught to keep house for him—if house it could be called.
In due course she had grown into the custom of accompany-
ing him to the town with his load of furze; still later, whenever he was busy working for the neighbouring farmers
at the harvest or ploughing, she was become venturesome
enough to undertake herself the delivery of the furze
branches at the potteries. She would start off before the sun
had risen, would pilot the ass and cart down the rough mountainy *poirsin,* along the white roads, and, at last, through
the cobbled streets of the town; would look, it seemed, neither to right at the sailormen nor left at the 'prentice potters,
but make straight on for one or other of the yards—there
were many of them then—would sedately receive the pay-
ment, would make her household purchases, always at the
traditional shops and in the traditional way, and arrive, often
times late at night, at the lonely cabin in the hills with
a mouthful of gossip for the sun-burnt, sun-drowsed exhausted man stretched along the settle patiently awaiting
her, his pipe in his mouth. He was not sharp enough in eye
or brain to notice that those visits were having more and
more attraction for the rich-blooded ripening girl. Her lips
were girlish, soft, and full; she had a tender grace and innocence about her, her brows were light, well-shaped; her
eyes timid and as dark as berries. She could not speak without blushing. Reared apart from womenfolk, she felt awkward when alone with them. She feared their questioning.

Forty years ago, then, after a long day's threshing in Pierce Fielding's barn, Tadhg Kinnane lay stretched in that patient attitude on the settle awaiting his daughter's return from the town. He saw the dusk thicken, the bats make their own of the sky, the earth darken, grow heavy and cold after the going of the sun; and then, one by one, he watched the stars coming into the heavens silently, silently. From the settle it was that he saw the night fall. At last he arose slowly, and slowly went out, sitting on a block of wood by the door. The pale wide glare of the afterlight startled him, so frank it was, so untender. Yet the coolness, after the labour of the day, found welcome in his limbs; he stretched out his legs, rested his back and head against the wall, and sleep fell on him.

When he awoke, suddenly, as if a whirring bird, with a cry, had struck him one stroke, a dark-blue silent night, gemmed with stars, was standing upon the earth. His hands were cold, and a soundless wind was feeling softly at his features. It was some moments before he realized that the fear he felt all about him, like a chilly, invisible garment, was due to his daughter's delay in the distant town. He groped his way into the hut, making for where the last spark of fire was still visible among the ashes; this, with the fire-wheel, he fanned up vigorously, indeed passionately. As suddenly he stopped and glared at the clock's face: it was ten minutes past one. It could not be so late, he thought; but from far away he heard a calf roaring, and the cry shook the heart in him, for it opened the spaces of the silent night, made it seem vast and lonely, vacant of any living soul to comfort one in trouble. No, it could not be so late, he reasoned with himself, yet again came that unrestrained cry of animal distress; and he felt he could not wait any longer. He plunged the candle into the fire, and set it lighting on the dresser. He reached for his coat, it hung on a hook in a roof timber, and as he flung it on he suddenly stretched an ear for other sounds that he fancied he had caught—the jolting of the ass cart as it made up the difficult, rocky passage towards the house.

"Ah!" he breathed, and the comfortable warmth of anger began to replace the chilly fear within him. Oh, he would speak to her, he would speak to her, and never again would she go alone into that cursed town of tradesmen and sailors. He buttoned his coat hurriedly, it would show her what he had been about to do; and, waiting, he stood on the threshold, alert, stiffened up, filling the opening, the night-blue sky before him, the glowing interior behind. Again, and more clearly, he heard the homely, drowsy, unhurried rattling, and he drank comfort from it. Then it ceased. But almost at once, again began. Once more stopped, for some time too. Once more began, stopped once more. "God guide us, God guide us," he breathed, and made hurriedly down towards the rambling, uncertain noises. He found the cart dragged obliquely across the passage, the ass cropping the long dew-cold herbage by the edge of the way.

As for his daughter—she already was far on the sea in the arms of the wild young skipper of the *Calliope*.

Tim Tobin, then, had said the word that had renewed for them the story of Kinnane's far-off day of trouble. Bitter and all as old Tadhg was, he had suffered his share, and had, as they said, shrunk into himself, closing not only his mouth but his heart. When one is come to that what is left except to bend upon the work of the day? And this he did. He would labour for the farmers round about, sometimes rising at dawn and travelling ten or fifteen miles to a harvesting or ploughing, and, come home, would be heard late in the night hacking and hewing in the furze thickets by the river bed or along the hills. He took on pottery after pottery, and kept them going, and neither the driving sea winds nor mountain floods nor rains ever hindered him or even delayed his coming to them at the right time. They it was that failed him, one after another giving up the ancient way. By this time, however, himself was getting old, was now more than eighty years; and for one so old the hacking out and the gathering and the piling of one load of furze branches was a full week's work.

"Do you know, I'm sorry for the old creature—in a way."

"Um, um, you needn't then. He won't starve."

"That's true. Still, what'll he do with himself?"

"Lie down and die; and indeed they're a long time waiting for him, his people in Ardmore."

"Will he come to-day, I wonder?"

II

As if unaware of any change whatever, the old man dragged his little donkey, rather viciously, one thought, into the yard. Animal, tackling, furze branches, cart—and then the old man himself—face, whiskers, hair, hands, clothes— they all were of one texture and one hue—a rough, hodden grey upon which the dust of the long distance he had come was scarcely noticeable. As always, the animal made to swerve to the left where, it remembered, long tufts of bluish grass were to be cropped between the cobble-stones; and, as ever, the old man snarled at it, "Come on, you!" Then, "Whu-ee!" "Whu-ee," his hard old lips blew out, and he threw the reins carelessly on its back. He stopped suddenly, his head down, even more than usual, his brows bent, even more than usual, to that intensity of purpose by which he seemed to live. At last, fixing his thought, he hobbled forward quite briskly towards the open-air stairs which led up to John Connole's office. But again he paused, hesitating for a moment; and, as precipitately as he had gone from it, made back to his cart, from which, hurriedly, he began to fling the furze branches off about the yard. John Connole, who must have seen him, came on to the wooden platform at the head of the stairs: "Take them up again, take them up, I say. And be off

with you, be off with you, you old deceiver. You were told
not to bring them."

The old man stopped as he pulled one from the pile; he
held it in his hand, awkwardly, like a defeated flag; such
words he had heard before in other potters' yards. Timidly,
quietly, he put the branch on the ground. "Take them up, I
tell ye. Didn't I tell you I was done with you? Be off with
yourself."

John Connole turned his back and went into his office. The
old man raised his eyes towards where he had been speaking
on the platform.

A little group were standing under a low wide archway:
the autumn sun was playing about their feet, not on their
heads or faces: "There you are, Tadhg. There you are," one
of them called to him, not roughly. He could think of nothing
else to say.

John Connole's son came across the yard. He was well-
dressed, well-combed. He had some papers in his hand. He
was puzzled for a moment to see the old man slowly replac-
ing the branches on the car: when he understood, he made
a gesture with the papers towards the group in the archway:
"Give him a hand with them," he said, and with the lightness
of youth in his limbs bounded up the wooden stairs.

The men began quickly to fling the branches on to the cart,
old Tadhg looking at them suspiciously. For them during the
long, long years he had always been little more than a butt
for their joking; they would begin again at any moment, he
felt; but no; they helped him to swing the cart about on the
rough cobble-stones, to set it going, and all without one word
of impatience. They then drew back, they had played their
part. He peered at them, still suspicious, but, making sure
they had no thought of gibing at him any more, he took a step
towards them; "Whisper," he said, "did ye ever hear this?"
and he hissed out an Irish saying, which, translated, is "pity-
ing the dead and the dead laughing!" They could only keep

their silence, staring at him. And he looked back at them, and smiled!

He grabbed the mouthpiece and led his swaying, carelessly built load through the gateway and out into the traffic of the main street.

III

It took him only a moment to make up his mind as to what he should do. He turned down a narrow sunless street of long-deserted warehouses. At the farther end was a glare of light—the wide sky, the bright waters of the estuary. He made straight for the edge of the jetty, dragging the donkey after him with a callous vigour, its head screwed sideways up. He swung the cart about until its tailpiece was towards the waters. Then, muttering and growling he began, still with something of a false strength in his limbs, to pitch the branches into the sea.

If he had drawn his cart in at any other point of those all-too-spacious jetties, he might have finished without interruption, but now, suddenly, he heard, "Look out!" shouted at him in an un-Irish accent. A sailorman with a noose of stout new rope across his guernsey, around his shoulders, was coming towards him laboriously: pressed forward at a sharp angle, his thin and worn shoes showed the play of the feet within them. It was not he who had shouted: it was another, whose duty it was to lift the rope over whatever quayside debris lay about. Again, this man shouted "Look out! Look out!" and failing to raise the cable high enough above the cart, about half the load was swept off on top of old Kinnane: when the rope had passed by, himself, too, had been thrown and was sprawling in the midst of the branches. He had to turn on his face and hands to rise up. He did so as if there were need for haste, as if he had no time to think of what had befallen, or of the wet rope, the labouring sailorman, or the ship that like a dazzling vision was gliding to its moorings.

He resumed without a thought, it seemed, and with the same
surly vigour, his task of pitching and kicking the branches
into the water. The last he flung in with all his strength.
"Take them with you, me fine salt water," he snarled, and
turned away. He at once began dragging his cart from the
quayside. The men on the ship, some of them standing with
mooring cables in their hands, thought doubtless that he
had been fulfilling some daily task and now was setting off
for home. He did not seem to have given one glance at the
ship: her spars were bright against the rich blue of the sky;
all about her were gleams, points of sun-fire, lines of light.
One glance perhaps he had given her, no more, when, sitting in his cart, he started for his lonely nest in the hills.

IV

How many, many hundred times he had thus in the gathering twilight made homewards! The falling night, the cool
airs, the silent winding road, showing dimly before him, the
rocky heathery hills, now closing in on his path, now opening out again, all the time, however, rising higher and higher,
growing darker and darker—it was easy for him in such surroundings to forget that this was the very last of all such jour-
neys: that he would never see the potteries again. And so,
now wide awake, shouting and pulling at the little animal,
and now drowsing into sleep, his head bobbing and his hands
hanging limp, resting on his knees—on and on he journeyed,
mile after mile. His voice was sometimes heard: "Go on, go
on, can't ye," and no weakening seemed to have overtaken
it. But, swinging around into that rising, stone-strewn, winding passage that led to his house, he suddenly felt afraid and
cold and lonesome. Only a dismal and empty hut lay before
him—as if it had not been empty and dismal for more than
forty years! A cold and empty house! but as suddenly he saw
out before him the ever-rising masts of a sailing ship, her
spars, her cordage, shining in the sun! "Go on, can't ye!" he

called out bravely, with a new ring in his voice, and from that until he threw the reins on its back, he gave the animal but little peace.

He removed the mouthpiece and left the ass to its haphazard grazing, the cart still tackled to it.

Meanwhile he had lit a candle, had closed the door, and soon was searching and poking in all the holes and corners of the room. Little cries broke from him. Sometimes he stopped, listening. He climbed up on chairs and fumbled at the roof timbers. At last he satisfied himself that no more remained to be done. In the middle of the place half a loaf of bread was hanging from a rafter by a string: it was his way of baulking the rats of it. From this he broke off some chunks and began hastily to chew them, still moving about as if unable to rest. He suddenly quenched the light, locked the door behind him, and made once more for the cart. He restored the mouthpiece, sat in brightly, and vigorously urged the animal back towards the town. It wanted an hour to dawn. "Ah! ah! ah-h-h!" he breathed out, showing his teeth —a cry that was full of triumph.

When he once more entered Youghal town, the pale morning was playing upon it; nevertheless, everything was still fast asleep, churches, shops, and houses deep in their dreams. Not a sound, not a movement—no door, no window stirring, no blind raised. The rattling of the wheels, even old Tadhg himself noticed how sharp and loud the sounds were. He was glad to turn once again into that deserted lane among the vacant warehouses. Again he made for the jetties. He tied his beast by the reins to some iron bars in a window frame. He hobbled forward, as with purpose, towards the dreaming ship. Silent she was, disdainful, yet his heart filled with warmth as he gazed up at her. Seagulls were flying about her topmasts, gliding and wheeling, crying out sharply their melancholy notes. Her grey-painted side was high above his head: he had not foreseen the difficulty of waking so huge a mass into life. But soon he noticed that a young sailor-man, smoking quietly, lazily, had been watching all the time. By way of greeting he raised hand and stick to him. He was afraid he might suddenly disappear into the depths of that huge contrivance. He drew nearer, hobbling, "Whisper," he said, cautiously beckoning the sailor to come closer—"Whisper, what's the name of her?"

"The name?"

"Yes, her name, what's on her, the ship?"

"The *Hispaniola.* 'Tis all along her."

"The *Calliope?*"

"No, the *Hispaniola.*"

"Whisper, whisper now: are they after changing it?"

"Change what?"

"The name of her. For why did they change it?" He was whispering up, his left hand at his mouth.

"They haven't changed it. *Hispaniola,* that's the lady's name."

"Ah, ah, I'm telling ye now, whisper, 'tis the *Calliope* she is. Isn't it I that should know that? 'Tisn't so easy to deceive me. The *Calliope*—and the Master—Captain Hinchion—that's the name. Look now, like a good boy—go in and tell him there's one here would like to make speech with him—and, whisper, 'twould be no harm to tell him that he won't be sorry at all if he's said by me. Go on now."

"But he's not aboard, your Captain Hinchion; he never was." As he spoke in his somnolent voice the sailor raised his eyebrows, his two hands, the smoking pipe in the fingers of one of them, held loosely.

"He never was," he repeated.

"Ah, he's not. He's not. You tell me that?" Perplexed, he stared piteously at the sailor. "*Calliope,*" he whispered again, in a sort of staring vacancy.

"No, *Hispaniola,* Portland, Maine."

The old man waved his hands with sudden joy.

"Portland, Maine—that's it. A hundred times they said it to me, 'tis there I'd find her."

"Was she from there?"

"Portland, Maine, Portland, Maine."

"Hold there a while now, will you?"

"No, no; stop! Come back."

"I'll be back presently."

"Ye will?"

"Certain."

He vanished from Tadhg's eyes; but the old eyes never shifted; they were fearful the sailor might not return. When he did return he was accompanied by an oldish, bleareyed, scrubby-bearded seaman, vicious-looking, scowling. His limbs were twisted with rheumatism. He fastened his gaze on Tadhg:

"The *Calliope?*" he muttered huskily, absently, his weary worn-out voice offending the freshness of the morning.

"Yes, yes."

"Portland, Maine?"

"Yes, yes."

"Captain Hinchion?"

"Hinchion—young. A bold lad. A bold lad."

"Right you are. I seen her often. I seen her in Portland, Maine. In Caleta Buena. In Sydney. . . . She went . . ."

He stretched his hand out over the ship's side, he lowered it slowly, the fingers wide apart one from another. "She foundered. Crew, Cap'n, Cargo. Cap'n's wife. All of 'em. All."

"They were drownded? All drownded, ye're saying?"

"You have it," he nodded affably.

The old man glared at him, his jaw hanging foolishly. The seaman took no notice; he raised his head: calculating how long ago it was since the *Calliope* had foundered, he was, unseeingly, staring into the windows of the little town, blindly, although every one of them was a living torch against the sun.

"It's forty years ago."

"Forty?" Tadhg repeated, in a dull and stupid voice.

"Forty, I said," the seaman rapped out at him. He was a chronicler of the seas. Tadhg's head swung up in answer: "The Captain's wife . . . she was my daughter. Maybe now, ye wouldn't believe that?"

Their eyes were fixed on him. There was something like a snarl of victory in his way of saying the words; and something like disdain in his abrupt turning away from them.

The young man laughed quietly. "Queer old thing," he said; but the other flung a string of filthy words after the retreating figure.

V

The spark of fire the truculence of the sailor had induced in old Tadhg lived but a moment; in a sort of stupor he got into his little cart and, almost without thinking, set out from the still-dreaming town towards his home. He had lost a whole night's sleep and, bright morning though it was, he had gone only a little way when his head dropped on his breast. It did not matter. Often and often before it had happened to him. All those who travelled that road were acquainted with him; had known him even in their childhood. To see him pass with his head fallen on his breast gave them scarce a thought. It was a little group of stranger tinkers that at last gathered about the cart, waking him up and telling him he had better be careful. Their wild faces, sun-dark, dirty, passionate, were about him in a ring. He stared at them stupidly. A middle-aged, bedraggled woman, with a child at her breast, folded into a shawl, was still shaking him, fearing he would drop off to sleep again. "Good man," she was saying, "You'll come to mischief, you'll come to misfortune. For the love of God mind yourself. 'Tis many a good man met his death and he going the road like that."

He gathered his wits. Anyone who had known him for

the past forty years would, as answer to her words, have expected from him a snarl, nothing else: but no, his voice sounded weak, uncertain of itself:

"And, *a laogh,* 'twould be all one. 'Tis how, whisper, *a laogh,*" he drew the woman towards him away from the others. " 'Tis how, they used to tell me they always come home in the end, and they broken, and every hand raised again' them, and they dark in themselves, and like a dirty slut upon their father's floor." He raised his head and looked at her straight in the eyes: "Let me tell you, let me inform you, 'tisn't like that she'd be with me, 'tisn't, 'tis not so, far from it, but in silks and satins, with bangles and ear rings, and—and ——" Words failed him, and he gave up, with an impatient gesture, the attempt to find them. "Whisper, what a mistake they were making! 'Tis I could dress her out. 'Tis so. And, whisper, not a soul knew it, not a soul knew it—and I laughing at them! Laughing at them in my heart of hearts! All the years of my life, laughing at them in my heart of hearts!" And he shook his head with satisfaction to think how he had been laughing at the world all the years of his life!

The tinker woman nodded to show she understood, but indeed all she understood was that the old man was simple-minded and couldn't keep his thoughts to himself. Suddenly she saw all his strength go from him, saw him trembling and trying to control his tongue. "But 'tis all one now"; he began to glawm his breast. "My heart," he said, "is a cage without a bird, I'm an empty sack! There is no spirit in me any more, nor strength nor life nor anything. But God's Will be done, the Will of God be done," he gathered up the reins weariedly. He did not care how long the road was, nor how cold and lonely his cabin.

The tinkers drew away from him, moving quickly on. The woman began to speak: "He's very old, that poor creature is. I didn't notice it at first. But I'd say he was a firm man in his day. A firm man. And he had the look of a miser. He was laughing, he said, in his heart of hearts. Look at that now—his heart of hearts."

But even as she spoke she was racing ahead eager to catch a glimpse of the town they had been making for since the break of day. Her bare feet as they swiftly padded along threw up clouds of dust from the sunny roadway.

The donkey cart meanwhile went on towards the distant hills, aimlessly, it seemed, straggling about the road. Every now and then the grey old head of the drooping figure in it would move from side to side, and "Vo! Vo! Vo! Vo!"—the traditional Irish cry of sorrow—would break from the lips. Sometimes the cry was loud and unrestrained; sometimes smothered, only a groaning.

Rock-of-the-Mass

....

I

D UNERLING EAST was its name, the model farm in all that countryside. Only after many years it had come to be so; and Michael Hodnett, the farmer who had made it so, lay fast asleep in his armchair on the right-hand side of the front door. As of its own weight his big strong-looking head had sunk itself deep into his deep chest. The sunshine of the October afternoon was depositing itself lavishly upon him, thickening upon him, it seemed, while slumber bound him there, so huge and lumpish, so inert, so old and fallen. Dunerling East just now was looking more model-like than ever before. The house itself had had all its sashes, its doors, its timber work painted afresh; its blinds and curtains had been renewed; its ivy growths trimmed; and the whole farm, even its farthest fields and screening thickets, spoke of the same well-being, the same skilful management. The sleeper might lawfully take his rest, his spirit had so indisputably established itself everywhere within the far-flung mearings. Even were he to pass away in his sleep, and stranger folk, as reckless as might be, to come into possession of the land, many years must needs go by before Dunerling East became hail-fellow-well-met with the farms round about it, shaggy and scraggy as they were, waterlogged in the bottoms and bleached or perished on the uplands, unsheltered by larch or beech.

All this cleaning up had been done in preparation for the
first coming together, after many years, of all or nearly all
that were left of the family. The arrival of Stephen Hodnett,
the third youngest son, from the States had been the occa-
sion. He had brought with him his young wife, and, as well,
an elder sister of hers, a young widow, for whose distraction
indeed the voyage had been undertaken. Of all the sons of
the house this son, Stephen, perhaps had done best: he was
now manager of a large bakery store in New York. But the
brother next to him in years, Finnbarr, had done well too.
He was come, also accompanied by his wife, from Kerry,
where he managed a very successful creamery. The son to
whom the care of the farm had fallen, to whom indeed the
farm now legally belonged, Nicholas by name, had main-
tained it in the condition to which his father, this old man
asleep in the chair, had brought it; perhaps he had even bet-
tered it, but, of course, the land had been got into good heart
long before it fell to his turn to till it. Nicholas, though older
than Stephen or Finnbarr, had never married: he would wait
until his father's death. The only other son of the house was
up in Dublin—Father Philip Hodnett, a curate in St. Mul-
tose's parish. He was the one living member who was not at
present in Dunerling East. Within the house lurked somewhere the eldest living of all the old man's family, Ellen, the
second child born to him. She looked old enough to be the
mother of those mentioned, even of Nicholas, the eldest of
them. She was sixty and looked more. Her cheeks were thin
and haggard, colourless, her hair grey, and her eyes stared
blankly at the life moving before them as if it were but an
insipid and shadowy thing when compared with what
moved restlessly, perhaps even disastrously, within the laby-
rinths of her own brain. On her the mothering of the whole
family had fallen when Michael Hodnett buried his wife in
Inchigeela.

From the feet of the sleeping figure the ground fell

away downwards to a bracken-covered stream. Beyond the bracken it rose again; much more suddenly however, so suddenly indeed that the red earth showed in patches through the tangled greenery. Those reddish patches looked like corbels supporting the cornice-like ledge of the upward-sloping grazing grounds above. Just now, along that sun-drenched ledge, a procession of shapely deep-uddered cattle was moving from left to right, the beasts in single file or in pairs or groups, deliberately pacing. Thirty-one milkers were to pass like that, making for the unseen bridgeway across the stream in the hollow. Presently they would dip from sight and again be discovered in the tree-covered passage trailing up towards the milking sheds, the rich sunshine catching their deep-coloured flanks and slipping swiftly and suddenly from their horns and moving limbs. Anyone who had ever come to know how deeply the sight of that afternoon ritual used to thrill the old man, now so sunken in his sleep, could hardly forbear from waking him to witness it.

Behind the cattle sauntered Nicholas. His head was bent, and in his right hand a sliver from a sally tree lazily switched the cattle along. Although a working day, he was dressed in his Sunday clothes. His gaiters were new, rich brown in colour, and had straps about them; his boots also were new and brown. All day since morning his visitors, his brothers Stephen and Finnbarr and their people, had been away motoring in the hills towards the west—around Keimaneigh and Gougane Barra—and he had found the idle day as long as a week. "Stay where you are," he had said to one of the labourers who were digging out potatoes in the fields behind the house; "stay where you are, and I'll bring them in," and he was glad of the chance to go through the fields one after another until he was come to where the impatient cattle were gathered, anxious and crying, about the fastened gate. Their time for milking was overdue, and they needed no urging towards the sheds. When they were safe across the bridge he left them to themselves: by that time the first of them were already head-bound in the stalls. Closing a gate behind them he made diagonally up the sloping field. At his approach his father suddenly raised his head.

" 'Tisn't Sunday?" he said, and then, recollecting himself: "They haven't come back yet?"

"Any moment now," Nicholas answered. He then turned his back on him and gazed across the countryside where a couple of roads could be picked out. The weather had been very fine for some weeks and little clouds of sunny dust wavered above them.

"Are the cows in?"

"I'm after bringing them across."

"Is Finn after looking at them?"

"Yes, he'd get rid of the Kerry, he said."

"Didn't I tell you! Didn't I tell you!"

He had filled up with passionate life. As he blurted out the words, he raised his heavy stick in his blob of a hand. Nicholas glanced away from him, and again searched the countryside with his eyes:

"They won't be long now: 'tis as good for us to be going in!"

He put his arm beneath his father's. He lifted him. The old man's right foot trailed uselessly along the ground. But his thoughts were on the cows:

" 'Tis often I do be thinking on the two beasts we had and we coming hither from Carrig-an-afrinn. Scraggy animals, scraggy, splintery things."

II

Mrs. Muntleberry, the young American widow, and her sister, Stephen's wife, were both thoughtful gentle women; it was plain in their quiet eyes, their quiet faces. After the meal, homely in its way, but good, they now sat bent forward earnestly staring at the old man who was keeping himself so

alert and upright in their midst, ruling the roomful with
word, gesture, glance. Of his power of work, of his down-
rightness, they had, of course, often heard from Stephen: in
Stephen himself they had found something of the same character: until today, however, they had not realized how timid
in him were the strong traits of his father's character. They
had been motoring in a world of rock-strewn hillsides; they
had swung into glens that struck them cold, so bleak they
were, so stern-looking even in the softest tide of the year.
Carrig-an-afrinn they had not actually passed through: it
would have meant threading slowly up many twisting narrow hillside bohereens in which their car could scarcely turn:
perhaps also Stephen had not cared to have them actually
come upon the bedraggled homestead—little else than a hut
—from which the Hodnetts had risen. They had, however,
gone as close to it as the main road allowed them, had seen,
and felt almost in their bones, the niggardliness of life
among those hillsides of tumultuously tumbled rocks. That
wayfaring in bleak places had brought them to understand
Stephen's father; even if he were no different this evening,
had remained as he had been ever since their arrival—
drowsing between sleep and waking, mumbling old songs,
sometimes losing count of who they were—they would nevertheless because of this day's excursioning have more deeply
understood the tough timber that was in him. But all the evening he had been quite different. The names of old places, of
old families, had been in the air about him. He grew young
to hear them, to bethink himself of them. They had aroused
him. Stephen had forgotten many of them. He would say,
" 'Tis north from Inchimore," and his father had enough to
catch at: " 'Tis the Sweeneys were north of Inchimore. 'Tis
Keimcorravoola you're thinking of." And of itself either the
place name or the family name was enough to spur the old
man's brain to all manner of recollections. So it had been

with him all the evening, alert as they had never seen him,
a new man, and not a bit modest about his powers when
young, whether at fighting or hurley or farming. His stick
was in the air about their heads: and once without warning he had brought it down on the table, making them all
leap to their feet and grab at the dancing tea things—down
with all his force lest they should not clearly understand
how final had been the stroke with which he had felled a
Twomey man in a faction fight at Ballyvourney. And when
in speaking of some other ancient wrestling bout he referred
to his adversary's trunk, how he had clasped it and could
not be shaken off, the two women looked at himself, alert
yet lumpish before them, noted his body's girth and depth,
and felt that "trunk" was indeed the right word to use of
such bodies.

Finn's wife, the Kerry woman, was enjoying it heartily.
Her Kerry eyes, deep hazel in colour, were dancing to watch
the old man's antics, grotesque and unashamed, were dancing also to note the quiet, stilly, well-schooled Americans
opening the doors of their minds to comprehend adequately
this rough-hewn chunk of peasant human kind. The expression coming and going on the faces of the three sons, she also
enjoyed. She watched to see how they took every gross countryside word and phrase that would unconcernedly break
from the old man's lips. Her own Finn she held for the clever-
est of them because he had the gift of slipping in some con-
trary word that would excite his father to still more energetic
gestures or more emphatic expletives.

In time old Hodnett had exhausted the tale of the great
deeds of his prime: a gentler mood descended on him: "Like
you'd shut that door, or like you'd tear a page out of a book
and throw it from you, I put an end to all that folly and wild-
ness. Listen now, let ye listen now, this is what happened
and I coming over here from Carrig-an-afrinn."

III

He told them how on that day which of all the days of his long life stood most clearly before his mind, he had made swiftly home from the fair at Macroom. Michael, his eldest son, a boy of about sixteen years at the time, had hastened down from the potato field on hearing the jolting of the returning cart. As usual with him he examined his father's face. He was at first relieved and then puzzled to discover from it that his father had scarcely taken any drink during that long day of absence from home, of boon companionship in the town. More than that, his father was going about in a sort of constraint, as if he had had something happen to him while away, or had come upon some tidings which now must be dwelt upon within himself. Yet he did not seem gloomy or rough, and he could be gloomy enough and rough enough when the fit was on him. Often and often after a long day in Macroom, he had turned in from the road, flung the reins on the horse's back, and without preface begun to heap malediction on the head of the villain pig buyers from Cork with whom he had been trafficking. To-day he was different:

"Is Johnny above?" he questioned his son as he loosed the horse from the shafts. The boy nodded.

"Up with you then. Up with you while there's light in it."

The boy, climbing up to where he had left old Johnny, who was helping them to dig out the potatoes, was still wondering over the mood his father had returned in.

"What is he after getting?" the labourer asked him.

"Four ten."

"He'd get more in Dunmanway last Friday."

"He's satisfied. He says he is."

Before long they saw himself coming through the gap. "What way are they up along there?" he asked them, nodding his head towards the sloping ridges they had been digging.

"Small enough then," his son answered.

The father stooped and picked up one of the potatoes. He began to rub it between his finger and thumb.

"They'll be different in Dunerling East," his son said, complacently tossing his head.

As if that were the last thing he had expected to come from the boy's lips his father looked sharply at him.

Dunerling East was the farm he had been for several weeks negotiating the purchase of. It was ten miles away towards the east, ten miles farther from the hardness of the mountains, the cold rains, the winds, the mists. In those ten miles the barren hills that separate Cork from Kerry had space to stretch themselves out, to die away into gentle curves, to become soft and kind. So curiously his father had looked at him the boy wondered if something had not happened to upset the purchase. He was not surprised when his father, peering at him under his brows, spoke to him in a cold voice:

"The potatoes might be better. The grass too. And the cattle. Only the Hodnetts might be worse."

Michael glanced at the labourer, then back at his father. He found him still skinning the potato with his hard thumb. But he could also see, young and all as he was, that his thought was not on the potato, big or little. The labourer had once more bent to his digging; and Michael, withdrawing his eyes slowly from his father's face, spat on his hands and gripped the spade: yet he could not resist saying:

"They're poor return for a man's labour."

He scornfully touched the potatoes hither and thither with the tip of his spade, freeing them from the turfy earth, black and fibrous. They were indeed small.

The father seemed careless of their size. He stood there, a solid piece of humankind, huge, big-faced, with small round eyes, shrewd-looking, not unhumorous. He said: "If I hadn't that fifty pound paid on it, I'd put Dunerling East out of my mind."

He turned from them and made for the gap through which he had come. They questioned each other with their eyes and then stared after the earnest figure until the broken hillside swallowed it up.

It was a soft, still evening. Here and there a yellow leaf fell from the few scattered birch trees growing among the rocks which, on every side, surrounded the little patch of tilled earth. A robin was singing quietly, patiently—the robin's way. The air was moist; and because a break in the weather seemed near, they worked on, the two of them, until they could no longer see the potatoes. Then Johnny straightened his back, lit his bit of a pipe and shouldered his spade. Together both of them, taking long slow strides, made down towards the house. Suddenly the boy said:

"Look at himself!"

They saw him standing upright on one of the numerous ledges of rock which broke up through the surface of their stubble field. He had his back towards them. He was staring downwards, overlooking his own land, towards the straggling road, staring intently, although little except the general shape of the countryside could now be distinguished.

"Is it? Is it him at all, do you think?" old Johnny asked.

" 'Tis sure," Michael answered. Then he cried out, sending the vowels travelling:

"Ho-o! Ho-o!"

His father turned and after a pause began to make towards them. Awkwardly they awaited him; they did not know what to say. He said:

" 'Tis at Carrig-an-afrinn I was looking."

Carrig-an-afrinn was the name of the whole farm, a large district, mostly a hillside of rock and heather; they were standing in Carrig-an-afrinn: but they understood that what he had been looking at was Carrig-an-afrinn itself—the Rock of the Mass, the isolated pile of rock by the roadside from which the ploughland had got its name.

They walked beside him then.

"I'm after hearing a thing this day I never knew before," he said, and then stopping up and examining their faces he added:

" 'Tis what I heard: In any place where a Mass was ever celebrated an angel is set on guard for ever and ever."

" 'Twould be a likely thing," the old labourer said.

"I never heard tell of it," Michael said.

"Myself never heard tell of it," his father snapped out.

" 'Twould be a likely thing," old Johnny said again, "remembering the nature of the Mass."

"Who was it told you?"

"One who was well able!"

The three of them turned and looked downwards towards the rough altar-like pile of rock where Mass used to be said secretly for the people in the penal days when it was felony to celebrate Mass in public. Only the pile of rock was visible, and that not distinctly, so thick the light had become.

"You know very well that Mass was said there hundreds and hundreds of times."

The father spoke to his son almost as if he had been contradicting him. He received no reply. Then he added in a suddenly-deepened voice:

"Likely that place is thick with angels."

The labourer uncovered his head without a word.

In stillness they stood there on the lonely hillside; and in the darkening rocks and fields there was no sound, except of small things stirring at their feet. After a few seconds, the farmer faced again for the house. Without thought, it seemed, he avoided the rocky patches. Indeed even at midnight he could have walked unperplexed through those rock-strewn fields. The others heard his voice coming to them in the dusk over his shoulder:

" 'Tis a strange thing that I never heard of that wonder until I'm just leaving the place for good and all. A strange thing; and it frightens me."

When they found themselves free of the fields and in the *poirse,* or laneway, that led up to their yard, he said again with sudden passion:

" 'Tis a small thing would make me break the bargain."

The boy flared up:

"A queer thing you'd do then."

"Queer!"

"It may be years and years before we have the chance of buying a place like Dunerling East."

He spoke the name as if that of itself were worth the purchase money.

"Carrig-an-afrinn is not a bad farm at all."

At this Michael burst out:

"Johnny, do you hear him? And he raging and swearing at them rocks as long as I remember—raging and swearing at them as if they were living men and they against him! And he praying to God to take us out of it before his eyes were blinded with the years. And now he'd stay in it!"

Of that incident and of the night that followed it, the old man, forty-four years after, remembered every detail—every word spoken and every thought that disturbed his rest.

IV

Having given them to understand all that has been here set down, he went on: "I tell ye, I didn't shut an eye that night, only thinking and thinking and I twisting and turning in my bed. When I looked back through the years and thought of what a poor place Carrig-an-afrinn was—there was scarcely a poorer—'twas little less than a miracle to have me able to buy out a big place like this—a place that had been in the grip of the gentry for hundreds and hundreds of years. And up to that I always thought that I had no one to thank for it but myself—the strength of my own four bones, but after what I was told in Macroom that day, how did I

know but that maybe it was in Carrig-an-afrinn itself the
luck was? and that good fortune would follow whoever lived
in it like good Christians, and that maybe secret friends
would help them, and they at the ploughing or waiting up
in the nights for a calf to come, or a young foal or a litter of
bonamhs itself? Who knows? Who knows? And what puzzled
me entirely was that I should be ignorant of all that until the
very day, as you may say, I was settled on leaving it. It
frightened me. While we were in Carrig-an-afrinn no great
sickness befell us or misfortune, except a horse to break his
leg or a cow to miscarry or a thing like that; and I thought of
all the strong farmers I was after seeing in my time, and they
having to sell off their places and scatter away with themselves into Cork or Dublin, or maybe to America itself. Sure
this place itself, if ye saw it when we came hither, the dirty
state 'twas in, the land gone back, exhausted, and the house
and sheds broken, everything in wrack and ruin—'tisn't with
a light heart ye'd undertake it. But of course only for that I
couldn't have bought it all at all. So I said to myself, and I
listening to the clock ticking at the foot of the bed, I'm un-
dertaking that big place, and maybe 'twon't thrive with me.
And if it fails me, where am I? That's what I said. If it fails
me, where am I? I tell ye, I was broken with thinking on it.
And all the time, and this is the queerest thing of all, I heard
someone saying, 'Carrig-an-afrinn, Carrig-an-afrinn. Carrig-
an-afrinn, Carrig-an-afrinn.' And not once or twice or
three times, but all the night long, and I thinking and thinking. Of course, there was no one saying it at all, only maybe
the beating of my own heart to be like a tune. But I was
afraid. I thought maybe music might come rising up to me
out of the *cummer*, and it thronged with angels, or a great
light come striking in at the window. And sure enough at last
I started up and I cried out, 'There it is! There it is!' But 'twas
no unnatural light at all, only the dawn of day breaking in
on top of me. 'Tis how I was after dozing off for a little while

unknown to myself, and I woke up suddenly in confusion and dread.

"That morning and I rising up my limbs were like wisps of straw. I was terrified of the long day before me, and that's the worst way a man can be. But when I came out and stood in the broad sun, and 'twas a morning of white frost, I drew in the air to myself, and I took courage to see my poor animals grazing so peacefully on the hill, just like what you see in a picture. If the big farms broke the men that were born to softness and luxury, Dunerling East wouldn't break me, and I reared hard and tough! That's what I said, with great daring in my breast.

"Not long after that we moved our handful of stock east to this place. I laughed to picture the two scraggy beasts, and all the deep feeding of Dunerling East to themselves. And that same evening myself and Michael, Michael that's dead, God rest him, went over and hither and in and out through the length and breadth of this estate and round by the boundary ditch; and 'tis a thing I will not forget till my dying day what he said to me, my son Michael, that same evening, and we killed from the exertion. He stopped and looked up at me before he spoke:

" 'Look,' he said, 'why have you your hands like that?'

"My two hands, clenched, and stiff, *stiff*, like you'd have them in a fight, watching your opponent, watching to catch him off his guard, or for fear he'd spring on you. That's how I had my hands. And 'twas natural for me to have my hands like that, for what I was saying to myself was: I'll break it! I'll break it! And I was saying that because if I didn't break it I was sport for the world. Like a bully at a fair I was, going about my own land the first day I walked it!"

In recalling the labours of his prime he had become a new man. When they looked at him they saw not the stricken old creature whose days were now spent in the drowsy sun, but the indomitable peasant who had wrung enough from the rocks of Carrig-an-afrinn to buy out Dunerling East from the broken gentry, and who then had reclaimed Dunerling East from its hundred years of neglect. When he could not find words to fit his thought his left eye would close tight, and one big tooth, that he still retained in his upper gum, would dig itself into his lower lip, until the struggling words came to him. And they noticed that his two hands had clenched themselves long before he needed them clenched to illustrate how it was he had tackled the reclamation of the sluggish marshlands of Dunerling East. His own sons quailed before him. The two Americans had drawn together, shoulder touching shoulder: they watched him across the table with wide eyes, their faces drawn. The creamery manager from Kerry dared no longer to put in his jocose word. He wished rather to be able to draw off the old man's mind from this renewal of the unrelenting warfare of his manhood. But no such word could he find: his father was abroad in a passion of fictitious energy: it would indeed be a potent word that could stay or hinder him. Every now and then the timbers of the heavy chair groaned beneath the movement of his awkward carcase. He was unconscious of it. It meant as little to him as his own exposing of the shifts, the meanness, the overreaching, the unintentional tyranny he had practised while he worked out his dream.

"My poor boy, Michael," he went on, "was the first to go. He was great for the work. For a boy that was slight and tender I never saw the equal of him. 'Twas how he had great spirit. A word was worse to him than a whip. When we'd be cutting the deep grass in the inches, half a dozen of us all in a line, and he'd fall behind, being young and soft, I'd say to him, 'Ah, Michael,' I'd say, 'God be with the little fields of Carrig-an-afrinn, you could cut them with a scissors'; that would bring him into line I tell ye. The poor boy. 'Twas pleurisy he got first; and we thought nothing of it: maybe we didn't take it in time. But what chance was there to be

taking him into Macroom to the doctor, or from one holy
well to another? The time he died too, it could not be a worse
time. Herself was after bringing little Stephen into the world
—and before she was rightly fit the harvest was upon us;
and 'twas the first real good harvest we got out of Dunerling
East. When I looked at it standing I said: ' 'Tis my doing and
my boy's doing, and my boy is dead!' But herself was better
than any man in a harvest field. Maybe she overworked herself. She wasn't the one to give in. The day she was laid in
Inchigeela 'tis well if I didn't curse the day I came hither
from Carrig-an-afrinn. Father O'Herlihy was standing by.
'The Lord giveth and the Lord taketh away,' he said, and
his hand on my shoulder, and 'twas all I could do to say
'Amen' to that. There I was with a houseful of them about
me and only herself, that poor thing inside, only herself to
do a ha'porth for them. I don't blame her for being as she
is—knitting, knitting, knitting, or looking into the fire and
thinking—I don't blame her at all. What she went through
after that, pulling and hauling and slashing and digging,
'twould kill half a parish. Up at four in the morning getting
the pigs' food ready, or the mash for the calves; and milking
the cows, and keeping the children from mischief. The only
other girl I had, she was second after Nicholas there, I lost
her just when she was rising to be of use to me. 'Twas a fever
she got from drinking bad water. And the two boys I lost
after that, one of them was the terror of the countryside. He
turned against herself inside; he was wild and fiery. Mind
you, he dared me to my face. He said what no son of mine
ever said to me. I won't repeat it. I won't repeat it. The eyes
were blazing in his head. The delicacy was showing in him.
The brains of that kind is a terror. He went off with himself
and left me in the lurch. And then he came back—one
twelvemonth after—and 'tis like herself inside he was. Only
bitter, and the health wasted. The same as any labouring
boy he walked in to me. Not a shirt to his back, or what you

could call a shirt. He shamed me, the way he was. And he dying on his feet. 'Twas a dead man was patrolling the fields for months before he took to the bed entirely. And I daren't say a word to him because he had a tongue would raise blisters on a withered skull. The other poor boy, his name was Laurence, was a handsome boy. Everybody used to say he'd make a handsome priest. But sure at that time I couldn't dream of such a thing. It takes a power of money to make a priest. He died of pneumonia, and not a thing to happen to him only a bit of a pain in his side. Only for that I hadn't time to be thinking on it I'd be saying there was a curse on top of us; but no, because year after year the produce was getting better and better; and in spite of all the sickness and deaths and funerals—and funerals are the greatest robbers of all—the money began to rise up on me, and I could get in the help when I wanted it—'tis often I had a score of men at the harvesting, besides what neighbours would come of themselves. Those there (he nodded at his three sons, all of them sitting with bowed heads, with pipes in their mouths, not daring to break across his speech)—those there, they only knew the end of the story. Ah boys, ah boys, the softness comes out of the hard, like the apple from the old twisted bough, and 'tis only the softness ye knew of. And then in the end of it all, the great change in the laws came about and I bought out the land and 'twas my own, as you may say. The day I signed for it, a sort of lowness came over me, and I remembered my poor dead boy saying, and he my first born. 'Look how you're holding your hands!' Let ye listen to me now; I cried down my eyes to my own self that night because herself was in the clay. That poor soul inside, you might as well be talking to a cock of last year's hay, dull with the weather and the sun, you'd only get 'yes' and 'no' for an answer. And the rest—those here—were too young. What I did was: to send over for old Johnny, old Johnny I would have helping me an odd time in Carrig-an-afrinn, to

come over to me, that I wanted him. God knows all I wanted
him for was to keep me in talk against that terrible fit of darkness and loneliness would fall on me again. He came over
and together we walked the land, every perch of it. He knew
what sort it was when we came hither, and 'tis he was the
man could tell the difference. What he said was, now, let
ye listen, let ye listen to what he said, and he only a poor
ignorant man: 'After all, 'twas only a rush in your hand!' Now
that was what a wrestler would say of another in the old
times, 'He was only a rush in my hands,' meaning by that
that he had no trouble in breaking him. That was great
praise and yet it couldn't rouse me for I was after walking
the land field after field; and one field I found was the same
as another. That's a strange thing to say. Maybe 'tis how I
was old and I coming hither. 'Twas in Carrig-an-afrinn I
grew up. There was never a man drove a handful of cattle
of his own rearing to a fair that hadn't some favourite among
them; and he sees the dealers come round them and strike
them and push them, and knock them about, and he knows
that they are all the same to him, that he sees no difference
between one and the other, except one to be riper than another, or a thing like that. And 'twas so with me. I walked
my fields and one was the same as another. There was no
corner of them that I could make for when the darkness
would fall on me. I knew 'twould be different in Carrig-an-
afrinn. And that's what I was thinking of when old Johnny
said to me that after all Dunerling East was like a rush in
my hands. I opened my heart to him. I told him I felt like
the steward of the place, and not like the owner of it. He
said 'twasn't right for me to be saying a thing like that, that
'tis down on my two knees I should be and I thanking God,
but that the heart of man was only a sieve. The very next
day and I still going about like that, counting up the great
improvements I was after making since I came in, and arguing with myself, and yet dissatisfied with myself, I wandered

up the hillside opposite, and whatever turn I gave or however the sun was shining, 'twas about four o'clock in the evening, I saw Doughill and Douse rising up in the west and snug away down at the foot of Doughill I saw a little shoulder of a hill, and 'Honour of God,' I said, 'if that isn't Carrigan-afrinn itself!' Let ye listen to me, I fell down on my knees in thanksgiving like a pagan would be praying to the sun! And from that day forward I had a spot of land to turn to when the black fit would fall on me. Mind you, 'twas a good time I found it, for while I was breaking the place and wrestling with it I didn't think of anything else, only to be going ahead and going ahead. But 'twas different when I could pay for the help, and I had time to look around, and the rent wasn't half what it used to be. Ah, the soft comes out of the hard, and the little lambs from the hailstones. If Dunerling East is a good property now 'twas many the hot sweat fell into the sods of its ridges. But sure them that could witness to that, they're all dead, except that poor thing inside, God help her; and 'tis she took the burden as well as the next."

V

His voice fell and the glow of exaltation vanished from his features.

"They're all dead?" Mrs. Muntleberry said, quietly.

"Dead!" the old man answered her, and having said it, his head kept on moving slightly up and down to some pulse in his brain.

"Then these," she said again, and indicated the three sons with her eyes, "these are a second crop."

"A second crop," he said, "except that poor creature inside."

They found it hard to break the silence that had fallen on them. Earlier in the evening both Stephen and Finnbarr had been, as one might say, themselves—Stephen, the bakery manager, a hustler, and Finn, the creamery manager, not unable to hustle also. But as the story went on, and, though they had heard it all in a fragmentary way before, they had scattered from the homestead without ever having made themselves one clear unified picture of what coming hither from Carrig-an-afrinn had meant for their father. They had never seen him clearly as one who would not be beaten, no matter who by his side fell worsted in the struggle. Only the oldest of them, Nicholas, the farmer, could recall any of the dead, and he was a soft quiet creature, strong of body, but inactive of brain. The one mood, however, had come upon all three; they were not much different from what they had been before they had scattered, from what they had been when Ellen would still them by whispering the one word: "Himself."

It was Finn who first rose. He went and lightly beat the inverted bowl of his pipe against the bars of the fire grate. Then drawing with his strong lips through the empty stem, head in the air, he took a few steps towards the window and drew back one of the heavy curtains. The colour, the glow had gone from the day. Instead there were now everywhere filmy veils of mist. Beyond the sunken stream the hillside looked near and the screens of trees, ash and beech, seemed tall and unsubstantial: in the twilight softness the homely features of farming and cattle trafficking were hidden away. The scene was gracious and tender. They all stared through the window.

"It looks fine, so it does," Finn said.

"It does; it looks fine," his wife added, letting the words die away.

The old man was listening.

" 'Tis what a traveller said, and he a man that had recourse to all the places in the world, 'tis what he said: that it had the appearance of a gentleman's place out and out."

Mrs. Muntleberry turned and let her eyes rest softly on his face:

"Still you liked Carrig-an-afrinn too?"

He lifted his head; such words he had not expected: "Ah, ma'am, ah, ma'am," he said, making an effort to move his trunk so that he might face her directly, "Carrig-an-afrinn, Carrig-an-afrinn, the very name of it, the very name of it!" And he stared at her with a fixity of expression that frightened her, stared at her in blank hopelessness of saying even the first word of all the words that rioted within him. He recovered. He swept his hand across his brow, toying with his hair. "They tell me Pat Leary, who's there ever since we came hither—there's only the one year between us—they tell me he sits in the *cummer* an odd hour at the foot of the rock where the Chalice used to stand. His work is done. He'll catch hold of plough nor snaffle no more, same as myself. 'Tis a great comfort to him to sit there."

She was sorry she had brought Carrig-an-afrinn back to his thoughts.

"The heart is a sieve," she said, watching him to see how he'd take old Johnny's word. But he was not so easily moved from mood to mood.

"You saw it to-day?" he questioned earnestly, "You saw it to-day?"

"We went quite close to it. Did we see the Rock itself? Did we, Stephen?"

Stephen said as boldly as he could:

"Oh yes, we went quite close to it."

"Ah, ma'am, Nicholas there, some day he's going to pack me into the motor car; and over with us to see it. It can't be long I have to stay."

Before he had finished, almost indeed at the first word, Nicholas had risen and quietly taken down a shabby-looking old violin from the top of a heavy cupboard that stood in the corner. While they all looked at him he tuned it without a word, and to him tuning was no easy task. Then he stretched his two long legs out from the chair and began to play.

The instrument was almost toneless, and the player almost without skill. He played the old songs of the countryside, going straight from one to another, from a *caoine* to a reel, from a love song to a lively rattle about cattle-dealing or horse racing. Nerveless, toneless, yet the playing was quiet; and it was the music itself, and not the instrument or musician was in the fiddler's mind. After a while this the Americans noticed. Then the scratching, the imperfect intonation, the incongruous transition from melody to melody disturbed them but little. He played on and on; and they were all thankful to him. The room darkened, but the sky was still bright. At last he lowered the fiddle, a string needed to be tightened. The others at once broke into talk. Mrs. Muntleberry was nearest to Nicholas. She had her eyes on the instrument. He noticed how at the word "Carrig-an-afrinn" which was again on the lips of the old man, her head had raised itself. He whispered to her, without taking his eyes off his task:

"He'll never see Carrig-an-afrinn again."

"No?" she whispered back, with a little gasp of surprise.

"Nor nobody else," he went on; "they're after blasting it away to make the road wider: 'tis how two lorries couldn't pass on it. I'm in dread of my life he'll find it out. 'Twould be terrible."

She turned her eyes on the old man's face. The music had restored him again to confidence. His eyes were glowing. He had re-established his mastery. "Let ye listen, let ye listen to me," he was saying.

Vision

....

I

J IMMY's mother, sharply, told him once again to keep
still; but how could he be expected to do that, ready for
the road as he was, dressed up as he was. A thick woollen
muffler bound him tightly together from his very lips to half-
way down his chest. Within that, again binding him together, was a double-breasted overcoat, while his little legs,
sturdy and strong, were bound in also, with gaiters. As he
ran about the flagged kitchen his gloved hands seemed to
herald his coming, the fingers wide apart. Dressed up like
that, how could he keep quiet? Besides, it was only four
o'clock in the morning, yet the whole house was up and
about. The fire was blazing. His mother was busy at it, or
was rinsing the teapot. The lamp on the wall was bright,
brighter than he had ever seen it. Whenever the kitchen door
opened a gush of cold entered, and he was astonished at the
darkness outside, it was so close up against the door. He
stared at it frightened; but when their man, Jackie, crossed
the haggard with a swinging lantern, and its beams brought
out the familiar objects, his terror changed to wonder, they
seemed so strange. And there was such silence. The horse
rattled his chains in it. The cart was being dragged from the
shed. Everything flowed in upon him. To add to the wonder,
their man rather noisily once again opened the door from
outside and, with his hand on the latch, thrust in his head

and said: "Listen, ma'am," and saying so turned and stared back into the darkness. The lamplight fell on his round head, his cheek, his shoulder, his hand; he looked like something cut out of paper. Jimmy made towards him, but his mother rapped out: "Be quiet, can't ye."

In the silence they heard a distant cart knocking its way down a treacherous hillside. The sounds were faint yet sharp; they widened the night for the boy: that cart, that horse, that man to be out in the middle of all that darkness. He put his gloved fingers against his lips to think of it. But Jackie said:

"That's Miah Sullivan, 'tis no one else."

"Isn't it early he's stirring?" the mother answered, adding with impatience: "Tell himself to hurry, I'm after wetting the tea."

When Jackie had gone Jimmy moved towards the door. His mother raised her voice:

"Look, there's your tea. Sit in. Drink it up or you won't go at all."

So he sat at the table, and while with his two gloved hands he held the cup dawdling at his lips, his eyes were staring through the doorway, his ears keeping track of the lonely sounds of the distant wheels. His father came from the haggard, and at the sight of him comfort and courage returned to him. With his father he would go anywhere. When he saw him cutting the cake he forgot everything except that very soon they would be on the road to the fair at Dunmanway. Besides there was no other fair till after Christmas. His father would buy him something, he didn't know what, he wouldn't tell him. But whatever it was it would be all his own; and he would show it to his cousins when they came from Johnstown.

In the cart with them were six pigs. Only for the old soap-box, which had been put beneath his feet, he could have felt them moving about. He was quite comfortable. They had no light, but his father knew the way; he knew where to duck to avoid the branches that sometimes swished along the cart, unseen.

II

A buyer had come. Jimmy saw him hoist himself on the wheel, bend himself down over the pigs, rouse them:

"They're not much," he said.

The boy was astonished. He flushed; he looked from the man to his father, but his father was only smiling; he heard him say quietly:

"Now, if you said they were handsome," and he saw him shrug his shoulders and look away. The buyer turned and made off, immediately came back and faced his father as if he hadn't said anything wrong at all! And his father didn't seem surprised. There was a little quiet talk, and then he saw the buyer grope for his father's hand, and slap his own right hand into it. He knew then the pigs had been sold.

After that his father put the horse, pigs and all, into a yard. The two of them then went into the house. The kitchen was full of people. They were all eating, sitting on long stools. There was noise, confusion, in the place, and he was glad when his father and himself were led into another room, a smaller room. After a while tea and rashers and eggs were brought to them on a tray. His father finished quickly, rose, and told him to sit on the sofa and wait until he came back: "I'm not forgetting at all, Jim," he said, and Jimmy knew he was talking about his present. When he reached the door the woman of the house looked in with him and said: "What fear is of him?"

He waited. He was glad he wasn't in the big room where all the people were; you could see the crumbs on their whiskers. But his father wasn't coming. After a long time the landlady again put in her head: "Are you all right?" she said. He nodded, and was just about to ask where his father was, but she was gone and the door was closed.

He sat quite still: he felt that if he stirred or moved about, somehow his father would not come back so soon. But he listened carefully to the voices outside thinking he might catch his father's voice. The woman once more put her head in. At once he was on his feet. "Where's my father?" he said.

She seemed surprised; she looked at him sharply. He heard her call out: "Molly, Molly," and as the servant girl entered she said: "Take Jimmy here over to Stephen's." Without a word, Molly, who was untidy, and flushed from cooking, caught up his hand roughly—he noticed it but it didn't matter—and hastened him across the street towards a very grand-looking doorway with a large round lamp above it.

"Did any of you see Ted Coveney?" she said boldly to the men standing on the steps.

A very tall man answered her: "He's inside at the meeting." Another said: "That's Ted Coveney's little boy," astonishing Jimmy, who never before had seen him. "Come on, Sonny," he said, catching his hand. Jimmy felt himself being led down a long tiled passage; a glass door was opened; he was steered into a crowded room. There was a long polished table with a great many men sitting around it; behind them others were standing along the walls. The man who had brought him in spoke to one of those seated; and Jimmy felt himself being lifted on to the man's knee. "Look at your daddy," was whispered in his ear.

At once Jimmy saw him; he was at the other side of the table away down to the right. And his father had seen him too, was smiling at him. He saw him raise a papered-up parcel, a long box it seemed to be. He knew it was his present. As he looked at it he heard a sharp silvery bell ring, ding ding, ding, ding, ding, and the noise lessened. He heard a man saying something about his father. First he said Mr. Coveney, but afterwards he said Ted Coveney, and then again Mr. Coveney. And he saw his father looking at the

speaker. Then his father began to speak, turning again towards the crowd; he was now looking up along the table,
looking almost at himself; but Jimmy soon understood that
though his father was looking in his direction he was not
looking at him or at anybody else or at anything else. It was
queer. And everybody was listening. Jimmy's eyes ranged
from face to face. Some of them frightened him: they were
cross-looking, they were staring fiercely at his father, their
mouths open. But his father wasn't cross-looking at all; he
didn't mind them. His head was tilted very much, his brows
were fixed, his eyes were intent, he was looking at no one,
just talking on and on, and although he was tapping the table with the corner of the box, tapping it very gently, Jimmy
felt his father didn't know that he had anything in his hand.
Suddenly there was some stir, a chair moved, and Jimmy,
terrified, heard some of the men cry out: "No, no; 'tisn't so;
'tis not," but the whole roomful cried against them: "Ye
know very well it is, it is; what fools we are."

His father had taken no notice, kept silent for a moment,
then went on talking, the box gently tapping the table. The
boy was puzzled. The room was now quite still, listening.
Suddenly his father stopped and said: "That's what I think
anyway." The boy saw him put the box this way and then
that way in front of him, staring at it, and at last take his
hand from it slowly, carefully, and fold his arms, and sit
back. A hubbub of talk began and someone stood up; but to
him no one would listen. Some were already leaving the
room. Jimmy felt himself being deposited in a vacant chair.
"Your daddy will be over to you in a minute," someone said
to him. There was a crowd pushing through the doorway.
Jimmy heard someone else say: "Ted Coveney is a good
judge, none better." He swung round but he could not pick
out who had said it. "A good judge, none better," he made
his own of the phrase, and he looked intently at his father.
He saw him in the midst of a group of men. They were asking

him questions. He was answering them. They were looking up at him.

III

The papered-up box contained a toy lorry, a real lorry, because nothing was missing in it. It had a cab with a seat within it; a steering wheel that turned the front wheels; those wheels themselves had rubber tires, you could smell the rubber. The back-board could be let down. That was how Tim Mason got the churns into his lorry. To note its wonders the boy felt himself trembling all over, his throat smothering. He held it in his two hands broadside to his eyes. He drank it in. He didn't know what to say until suddenly, in a sort of triumph, he found himself breathing out: "My father is a good judge," and he trailed his fingers along the toy. He would turn his cap back to front: Tim Mason always had his cap that way. He would race the lorry up the hill; he wouldn't blow his horn going up the hill, she'd make noise enough: Tim Mason had told him that. Coming down was different. He would blow his horn whenever he overtook the other lorries or a churn boy taking his milk to the creamery. You could bring meal in a lorry, a dozen sacks, he had seen them counted. You could take cattle in it, standing up. He'd put the young horse in it, with a halter on him.

As they jogged homewards darkness fell, and he began to feel cold. His father stopped the horse and wrapped an old coat about his son; his gloves he made him put on; and the lorry he stowed away safely beneath the soap-box. That certainly was the right place for it. How well his father had thought of it! Then surfeited with content, in a moment he was sunken in a deep sleep.

IV

When he awoke they were swinging into their own haggard. Familiar sounds had awakened him—the grinding of the wheels on the sloping rocks. Jackie was holding them a lantern, head high. He came forward, put it on a barrel top, took him from his father's grasp, and planted him on the ground. Through Jackie his father handed him his lorry. Jackie then caught the horse's head and led him in. He saw his mother coming from the house. She passed him as he stood there with his lorry in his hands, and made him no greeting. She went straight to the shed. She spoke to his father. He answered, his back turned to her. And then Jimmy heard her cry out angrily: "Only twelve pounds for the lot?" He heard no reply. Something else sharp and high she said, and turned, was making for the house. Again she hadn't seen him. He saw his father go into the shed. "My father is a good judge," he whispered, in a changed tone, however, as if he were remembering things. He stood there in the darkness puzzled, as still as a stone; his brows were fixed, his eyes intent, his head tilted; as for the toy in his hands, it might as well have been a bit of an old ashplant. He was called twice before he crossed the haggard without a word out of him.

Children

I

No, no; you'll not be the grandmother. I'll be the grandmother. Won't I Pidgie?"

"Well, I'll be the woman with the green shawl so," Maggie said.

"That was his wife."

"Whose wife?"

"The man who was dead. Who else?"

"And what'll I be, Pidgie?"

"Do ye remember the old one was taking her snuff? 'The Will of God be done,' she was saying. Do you remember her?"

"But what about me? I have no one."

Pidgie settled that, too: "You'll be the old man who had his handkerchief in his hat—see now?"

"But what'll I be saying? I don't know what he was saying."

"That's always the way with you. Because you always have someone by the tail. You don't know nothing. You must be holding out the hat in your left hand and catching hold of everyone with the other hand, and saying: 'When is the funeral leaving, maam? Oh my!'"

"That's easy, anyway. 'When is the funeral——'"

"No, that's not it. Look up in their faces. Open your eyes and look up at them. Wider. Wider, can't you? Begging like. 'When is the funeral leaving——?'"

"And what about the one had her hair down, and her blouse all open? And her face! Did you see her face? All *white!*"

"That was his sister. You don't know nothing either."

"And what was she saying—the white one?"

"I know," said Mamie, "Um, um, blimely end."

"You fool!"

"That's what I heard, anyway."

"Um, um, blimely end."

They laughed at Pidgie's mimicry.

"What was it so? You don't know yourself and you're laughing at me."

" 'Untimely end,' she was saying. What else?"

"And what's untimely end?"

"Because she starved him."

"Who?"

"His wife. The one with the green shawl."

"Oh!"

"And why didn't she answer her?"

"Didn't you see the old one with the snuff holding her back? Wasn't chalky-face only looking for fight? What else?"

"And what made her starve him?"

"She didn't starve him at all, you goose. Starve him, I'd like to see her. Sure they always say that."

"God, he was looking awful. I'll never go to a wake again."

"You said that the last time, too."

"Well, I won't. You'd think he was listening. Didn't I see him all night!"

" 'And hale and sound you left your mother's house.' "

"What's that?"

"That's what she was saying. 'Untimely end. Untimely end. And hale and sound——' "

"We'll begin now. I'll be the old granny."

"Well, fool about. 'Is it my poor man is dead or the little one? Is it my——' "

"You, now, Maggie."

"'Untimely end. Untimely end; and safe and——'"

"Liz, you now."

"What is it? Oh, I know. 'When is the funeral leaving, ma'am? Oh my! When——'"

"Now, Andy; you stretch out."

"I won't."

"You'll have to. How can we have a wake without a corpse? Now, no laughing out of ye. No one is to laugh. Only very mournful. Mournful. You're to be crying. Begin now."

From the next room came their mother's voice: "Be quiet, I'm telling ye. Is it rouse up the child ye will?"

She was about to go in to them when she was aware that Mrs. Deeling from the floor above had entered. She had stolen in quietly, as if she had come from a quiet place. Mrs. Buttimer, speaking in a low voice, said:

"How is she to-day?"

"Grand then. Grand. As happy as Larry."

"You have your hands full with her. She can't hold out much longer. God knows they're a great trial when they're so old."

"Wisha, there's no one hastening her out. I'll miss her when she goes, for all her figaries."

"Sure you'd miss an old chair."

"I don't mind at all only when I wake up in the night and not a stir in the house."

Mrs. Buttimer tapped at the door of the room where the children were having their wake. The voices quieted for the moment.

"In the middle of the night when there's not a stir, only herself gabbling away. To her little brother she do be speaking, and he dead this seventy years! 'Don't go near that one. She'll pick you.'"

"Who'd pick him?"

"Some old goose they had. And you know she says it like

this: 'Johnny! Johnny! Keep away. Keep away, Johnny. She'll pick you.' God knows, Mrs. B., you'd take your oath she had him by the hand."

"My!"

"Listening to her and I trying not to listen—that's the way with me. And I after hearing it all a hundred times over. And the whole world asleep outside. And the whole house."

" 'Twould be worse if the poor old thing was in pain."

"That's true, too."

" 'Tis thankful to God you ought to be."

"And I am; but 'tis cruel lonesome, I'm telling you; and some night I'll break down."

"You won't then."

"What was she doing and I coming down, do you think? Picking flowers!"

"My!"

"To hear the little old voice of her! Like a little bird. 'Here's a lovely one, now. Wait, now, and I'll get them red primroses. Wait now.' "

"Isn't it good to have her so kind."

"Do you know what I said to her? 'If it's flowers you want, you'll have to travel a mile or two from Coley's Lane, ma'am.' She only looked at me. You'd think she never heard the name!"

"Wonderful. Do you know, Mrs. Deeling, I never spent a whole day in the country. Would you believe that? A real day: waking up, and eating, and lying down. Never."

"No? Oh, when I married himself first I used often go down to the old woman's house in Caherlag. That's why I'm lonesome when she begins to ramble about it. It comes back to me: the little stream, the little donkey, the bluebells——"

In spite of the closed door the children's voices came into the room. Mrs. Buttimer said:

"Wouldn't they annoy you. They'll rouse him on me."

"They won't, then. I'm watching him. Look, he's laughing.

'Tis something in his mind."

"I often see him laughing like that."

The voices in the other room were strengthening:

"Untimely end!" "Untimely end!" "When is the funeral leaving, ma'am? Oh my!" "You starved him."

Mrs. Buttimer rose and tapped a little viciously at the door; and again the wailing hubbub quieted. Mrs. Deeling was bending above the cradle; she said, raising her head:

"Laughing away for himself. And look at the fist of him! Tisn't picking flowers he is, I tell you. But I'd better go up and see what the child above is at."

She turned to Mrs. Buttimer.

"Do you know, 'tis queer, when you think of it. That poor child of mine—if ever a woman had to struggle and to fight her way through the trials and troubles of this world, 'twas that poor thing above in the bed. Sickness and sorrow and death and hunger. And there she is now, picking flowers for herself in the fields!"

" 'Tis blest you are. Do you hear them inside?"

Mrs. Deeling said:

"If she's after dropping off I'll come down again."

"Do then."

She went out quietly, as if going to a quiet place; and Mrs. Buttimer, her head a little on one side, looked down on the face of the child, sturdy-looking in his dreams. She looked down on it long and steadily, thinking of nothing, too happy to think of anything. In spite of the hub-bub in the next room, the whole house, the whole world, to her seemed to be quite still.

The Lilac Tree

··

I N PIDGIE WHITE's backyard there grew a lilac tree. The
backyard was cobble-paved in parts; in other parts it was
simply dirt, wet, slimy, blackish. All the other yards in
that forlorn slum were not any different, only that some
were larger and others smaller. But not a single one of them
had a single living green thing to enliven it, let alone a blos-
soming tree. It was a pity that the tree grew just where it
did. If it sprang from the patch of cobble-stones in the centre of the yard, or if it grew beside the Whites' backdoor, all
would be well; but no, quite close to the wall that separated
them from the Tweedys' was where it was growing; where it
would always grow, for it was now too old for shifting. Because of the tree, the members of the two families had not
spoken with one another for years and years. On special occasions, it is true, they had spoken to one another across and
even through the party wall, and that with vigour and
haughtiness and contempt. To such communication silence
itself was preferable; and months of silence were sanely kept,
might never be broken in upon with noise, only for the way
the springtime would lay its spell upon the tree—temptation
that could not be resisted. Now that May was come, any
night now, the Whites might catch the sound of cracking
and tearing branches, and catching the sounds, must charge
helter-skelter down the stairs and out the door, only, how-

ever, to find in the yard darkness and silence and nothing
else: they would examine the fresh woundings by the light of
a candle, would mutter and growl and straggle back to bed
depressed but determined. They were a low lot, the
Tweedys, a lot of savages, as everybody knew.

In spite of that annual ravaging, however, and perhaps
because of it in some degree, their backyard treasure-trove
was paraded abroad whenever a chance offered. It was good
to see Pidgie bearing an armful of blossoms to the presbytery
of a May evening, or to some neighbouring tenement where
some poor corpse was laid out, or up some crowded stairway
of a morning where a young girl was being dressed to go out
to her marriage. Pidgie, therefore, thought it was quite natural that there should be some difference between herself
and all the other girls, whether they lived in Mason's Court
or in Thompson's Alley or in Mullard's Lane. Lesser triumphs
she also knew. To saunter quietly into a group of her com-
panions, to take her place among them, join in the chit-chat
and the tale-telling for a while, and then, unconsciously as
it were, to draw her hand from behind her back and delicately brush the tip of her nose with a single spire of blossom—well, that was something also.

Of a drowsy summer afternoon she slipped quietly into
such a group, and found them all tip-toe with excitement:
The Millings had drawn a horse in the Sweepstake! They
mightn't win £30,000, that was so, but since they had drawn
a horse they were sure of thousands anyway. Of all people
in the world—the Millings! the Millings of Mason's Court,
just round the corner. There was no doubt about it. Mrs. Milling had got a telegram. She had taken the name of the boy
who had brought it. Wasn't he the lucky boy? They'd give
him a hundred surely.

"They will! Oh, they will!" Pidgie White said, and with
great bitterness, for she, she felt, had more reason to be upset than any of the rest of them. The Millings were cousins

of the Tweedys, her next door neighbours. The Tweedys were low, were indeed nothing, but the Millings were lower, were still less. The Tweedys used to get them to tear down branches from her tree; they could swear then in the court that they hadn't touched it. Indeed it was the Tweedys used to feed them half the time, they were so utterly down and out. And they, the Millings, were now—why nobody could really understand what they were now. But whatever they were the Tweedys would share the triumph with them. A bit of a lilac tree would make but a poor show against what they were to come into. Its day was gone.

Mamie Horgan said that her mother had said that she was glad *she* hadn't won anyhow; because no luck ever followed the Sweep. Families were divided and broken up over it, her mother said; and anyway it drove people to drink, or the man went away from his wife or the wife from her husband, and some one of them was sure to end up in the asylum, her mother said. And anyway wasn't there always law over it? That was true anyhow: they couldn't remember the names, but there never was a draw without any amount of law following it. There was a curse upon it.

Pidgie White had an ear opened to all that: there was a grain of comfort in it.

And then Vesey Terry came along, bluff and hearty as usual.

"Good evening, girls. Good news, girls. Who's for Mason's Court? That's where the Millings' Millions are, isn't it?"

But then she changed her tone, for they didn't play up to that heartiness—she changed her tone and said:

"Did ye see the chap with the leather bag under his arm? Went down this way. He's after taking the whole lane. He told Mrs. Milling to smile. "Smile, ma'am, when I nods at ye," he said, and he nodded and she did *that*."

But they didn't smile. It wasn't fair to the whole place to have £30,000 go to the Millings. Not one of them but felt that. And Pidgie White was already thinking of certain remarks that would be given out, by way of no harm, in the yard next door. It was easy enough for Vesey Terry to joke about it, but she didn't live in the next house to the Tweedys and she wouldn't have to listen to such remarks.

Then Nonie Lacy came along, her eyes standing in her head. "Me da says there'll be heaps of law about it—heaps and heaps of it: there's twenty names on the ticket, sixpence a go."

"Oh!"

"An' me da says, before the night is out you'll see ructions in the Court and the guards coming and hauling them away; and me da says——"

But then Mamie Horgan raised her hand, stilled them with a gesture, and said in a low and breathy whisper: "Don't stir, one of ye. Not a stir——"

They then all looked where she was looking.

"Way for Lady Milling," she whispered, in a still lower tone.

Maisie Milling herself had turned the corner of Mason's Court, was coming towards them, at the other side of the street, however. She didn't look as if she feared heaps and heaps of law; one could not tell by her that the guards presently would be dragging her parents off to prison. Her small dark head, perfectly round, dainty even, nicely held up; her long neck, her long legs—although her left calf showed white where the stocking was torn—they were all of the greatest assistance to her. She was ladylike, no doubt about it. No lady was ever so serious looking or so composed. Her head was raised up, yes, but was well forward also, and her narrow shoulders leant up towards it somehow—very ladylike indeed. Her left elbow was close in to her side, her hand was poised, well-bent at the wrist, as if she was carrying a dainty reticule, although there was nothing at all in it; her lips were pursed a little, and her eyes were cast down, so that she

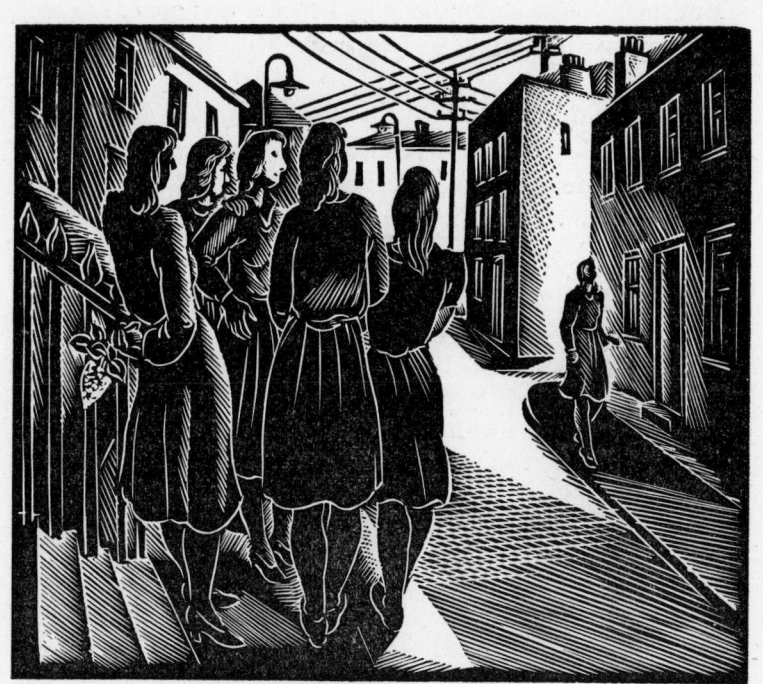

could see no one, not even if they stared at her.

There was dead silence, stillness, as she passed.

"Her business if of great importance," Mamie whispered, and Nonie added in the same low key: "She's paying a visit to her poor relations."

But their voices strengthened when she was gone.

"I suppose they'll take the Tweedys with them when they move——"

"Move where? Move into the filth of the law courts, and from that to the gaol—where else? Have sense, girl."

It was Pidgie White who spoke.

"Heavens, here she's back again."

Silence took them again, even a deeper silence; and held them while she passed them by, perfect again in pose and bearing. They felt it deeply. Even when she had gone some paces beyond earshot, they couldn't break the silence. But at last there was a stir; and Pidgie White was brushing their noses with the spire of lilac blossom and was saying to them with great conviction: "Smell, girls, smell, the air is putrid, putrid, girls." And her eyes were bright.

—As Benefits Forgot

. . . .

*In Iveleary they tell of this thing as having hap-
pened some seventy years ago.*

I

THE woman of the house, startled, sat up in the bed,
for old Mary had cried at her "Ma'am! Ma'am!" as she
shuffled in from the door.

"What is it, Mary? What's the matter?"

"Do you know who's below with me?"

"How would I know? Is it Michael? Is he after coming
back? I thought I said——"

" 'Tisn't Michael. I'd rather 'twas. 'Tis his sister—'tis Margaret. 'Tis herself and none other."

"Oh! Oh! Will you go down and give her what she wants.
Pacify her. Pacify her, Mary. I'll dress myself and go down.
If himself was here——. What time is it?"

" 'Tis better he's not here. 'Tis seven all out. She won't be
said by me."

"But try, Mary. Try."

"I can only do my best," and she turned towards the door.

The light was coming in. It was a windy morning, grey
and sunless, chilly, too. She cast a look at the sky as she heavily went down the stairs which led directly into the kitchen.
A low fire was on the hearth. She went towards it as if no one
else was in the room. That other person did not stir. She was

sitting at the end of the deal table; it lay along the wall beneath the one window. She was a wild-looking woman who, from her appearance, lived more on the roads and in the fields than under any roof tree. Her hair was strong, black, and was tangled roughly. Her skin was hard and dry with the weather. In her cheeks there were dark crimson stainings like one sees on bramble leaves in November. Her eyes, under dark strong eyebrows, were a fierce blue. She was passionate, impulsive, wary yet reckless. Her cloak was pulled tightly about her by the two fists hidden within it: the drag on it showed the meagre framework of flesh and blood. Her skirts went to the flagged floor, the same colour as it. One boot protruded from them, the same colour also.

She rocked a little because of her thoughts. Mary, building up the fire, placing the kettle on the hangers, passed to and fro before her; but the woman's eyes never rested on her. Without turning to her the old servant said:

"You won't refuse a cup of tea?"

"In this house I'll refuse a cup of tea. I'll refuse a cup of water—and that's less." Every phrase was emphasised by a quick jab of the wild head.

There was a long silence. The old servant tried again:

" 'Tis myself that's offering you the tea."

" 'Tisn't yours to offer."

After a long silence old Mary, still without looking at her, said:

"Don't be hard on herself."

That was a thing to be thought about. It was some time before Margaret replied, saying:

" 'Twas the master's will, not hers."

The woman of the house was coming slowly down the stairs.

"Are you having nothing, Margaret, after your travelling?"

"Not offending you, ma'am, I'm taking nothing."

"You know you can't see himself till nightfall. He's gone

since three this morning. Unless he sells the cattle on the road he won't be home till late."

"Unless he sells the cattle on the road," Margaret repeated, only in a voice so deep that it might have been a man's voice. It might have been her brother's voice, her brother, in whose hands the buying and selling of cattle for this house had lain for over fifty years. Mrs. Houlihan and Mary looked at each other with that same thought in their eyes. Then they both turned their heads again to the swaying figure whose face was towards the ground.

Mary placed a few tea things on the table. She had wet the tea. The mistress seated herself at the off end of the table from Margaret's place, and like her was turned towards the room. Mary sat with her back to it and between the others; through the window she could see the sky; the light of the young day was spreading in coldly on them.

Mistress and servant ate in silence. Indeed the whole place was silent except for the sudden stirrings of morning outside in the haggard—a dog nosing at the vessels, or the fowl scurrying from his sudden thrusts at them.

In that quietness, very unexpectedly, their visitor gave way to a fit of unrestrained sobbing, laying her arms on the deal board and burying her face in them.

The servant glanced at her mistress and shook her head, so bidding her not to interfere. But the woman of the house could eat no more. She rose and bent over the weeping figure, her hand upon her shoulder:

"You are sitting in his place; that's what you are thinking of. I'd rather see him there himself than you. He would be at peace there: and you'd be at peace, and I and all of us would be at peace. For you there's a place on the settle whenever you care to come to us; and if your brother Michael is here no longer 'tisn't I'm to blame; and don't blame the man of the house till you hear what he has to say on it, and don't blame him then either, for he done all for the best, and not to be rid of him or to save the bit he'd eat on us, only all for the best that his health might be spared to him, and the house spared from anger and arguing."

Sentence after sentence she uttered, chanting them out softly over the drooping head, close to the ear which the poor bedraggled locks half covered. But if the woman gathered in the sense of the words, she gave no sign. Yet she restrained herself, her passion had outwept itself, her head lay quiet on her arms.

Mary said to her mistress then:

"Sit down, can't you, and finish the bite. The care of the household is on you, and Margaret Cumeen understands all you have to keep you busy. She'll have no blame to you for finishing your cup of tea."

Margaret moved a hand in a deadish way to say that that was so. It also said that she attached no blame to the mistress of the house if her brother had been sent to the poorhouse after his half-century of work and care in this place. If the mistress's father was spared 'tisn't in the Dunmanway poorhouse her brother would be now among strangers and the riff-raff of the towns and villages, for he would not allow it. It was God's will to take him, and leave this place in the charge of this man, Houlihan, who came out of nothing, out of nothing, neither out of land nor out of breeding; and if he was after doing the hard thing and the bad thing 'twas kind for him. But what luck can be upon a house where such things are done? "Hannah Creedon," she said, addressing the woman of the house by her maiden name as if the new name Houlihan demeaned her, "Hannah Creedon, for the peace of your parents' souls and for the sake of the young children will be growing up in this place and hearing tell of how their father treated the man who had sweated his blood down into the fields of this farm, and fought for it with landlord and bailiff and policemen and agents; and with the bankers in their offices at their polished tables, for the sake of those will be coming to you, intercede with him for my brother, to bring him back and not to have him die in a strange place with strangers staring at him."

When she finished, her head, with its blue eyes wide open, was leant fiercely forward towards Mrs. Houlihan at the other end of the table; the eyes were staring at her, and the parted lips, the warm mouth, seemed to be staring also. But the servant, who had withdrawn from the table to the hearth again, sent another glance to her mistress to remain firm and not give way to her; so that the mistress turned from that eager, outstretched face and replied without looking at it:

" 'Twouldn't be of use. I did my best with him. Mary there did her best, too. If your brother, like another man, could curb his tongue, and take the instructions given to him by the master, whose place it is, there would be no quarrelling or clamper; but no, Michael couldn't do that, only have his way and his say, and cast it up to everyone morning, noon and night that without him the place was broken out long ago. So now, you understand, and 'tis no easy case to settle."

Margaret answered by saying her brother was an old man, seventy-three as they knew, and who'd mind what one as old as that would be saying, only let it go with him, for an old man's babble was like a child's babble. And how would he live in the place he was now, a man whose spirit was never broken? 'Tis a cruel thing, she said, to send an old man to a hard school; he'll draw down correction on his head before he knows what word he's after saying wrong.

There she stopped up, with her lips tightened together, for she was seeing in her mind all sorts of trouble overtaking him in his strange surroundings—a man who never had had what could be called a master over him until this stranger, this youngish man from another parish, had married into this house. In the poorhouse her brother would surely have a dozen masters over him, some of them as hard as John Houlihan, it was likely.

But Mary had poured her out a cup of tea. She implored her to drink. The woman of the house also implored her; but not so much as a glance would she give it. She spoke to herself:

"The hard words and the hard blows will keep him from remembering where he is; and that's better than for him to be thinking that 'tis there he'll find his death—and the place as cold as a prison cell."

She stood up at that. But the others rose, too, and came about her. "Where are you going?"

" 'Tis a thing I'm asking myself this moment."

"You're not going without breaking your fast?"

"I'm not hungry nor tired, though I have a right to be— only to be going——"

She gripped her stick, catching it up from the jamb of the door, and made out the yard with her eyes down.

In silence they saw her pass by the window.

"She'll go to Dunmanway; and that is best: I'm easy in my mind to know it," the servant said, going about her work. But the mistress, sitting again by the table, put the hem of her apron to her eyes and cried silently into it. No other word they spoke, the old servant thinking it well that the mistress should cry away her trouble, for she knew there had been but little peace in her mind since the old man was sent away. The mistress was thankful that old Mary kept her peace. She heard the wind going by the front of the house, harsh in the leafless thorn hedge beyond; but the wind did not matter: rain would be worse, with the man of the house selling his cattle in Macroom.

They were startled with loud cries from the haggard. There were sudden noises as of things being dragged and flung about. The hard clopping of a horse's hoofs—a horse let loose—came to them: they saw it go by the door, galloping wildly, its head in the air, no one on it, no one following it.

The cries came again: it was the new workman's voice: "Water! Water! Water!" he was shouting, "the haggard's on fire!"

They rushed out the door.

A moment after, Mary came running across the yard: she carried a large bucket in either hand. She stopped to swing one of them at the six milkers that were straying about: she would turn their heads towards the fields. The mistress rushed back into the kitchen. She dragged an old long coat on to her and got a piece of cord about it to keep it tidy. Her lips moving all the time, she made again for the sheds. They were around towards the east: the wind was not blowing from them to the house: that was well.

She was gone east but a little while when Margaret, in uneasy haste and confusion, came hobbling back to the house, wherever she had come from. Her stick shook in her right hand as she mounted the stone flag at the threshold. Her left groped for the jamb of the door. Within the house she raised her head as if for breath, her mouth wide open. She let herself sink on to the chair she had been sitting on before. She gave attention to the noises outside—the wind making the burning ricks roar; crackling, too, she heard, and the crying of the unmilked cattle which had clustered together by a closed gap. The servant, Mary, rushed in past her, groped by the dresser, snatched up one other bucket, and turning again towards the door, suddenly saw the silent woman in the chair. Instinctively she drew back the bucket as if to strike her; but strike her she did not. "You hound of hell!" she gasped at her as she went by her out to the salvaging. Margaret kept the word in her mouth, chawing it one might say; yet as she did so she heard horsemen outside; they had come up the hill at the sight of the flames. Her head shook weakly; and in a moment she seemed to slide helplessly down along her stick, her two hands loosening from it, down to the ground.

II

It was almost dusk before she came to herself. She was conscious of people moving about her, a great number it seemed, confusing her. She shook her head, gathering her recollection. Then she was conscious that they had all, as if in haste, drawn away from her, leaving her in a vacancy. She found she had been raised from the flags into the seat she had fallen from, a heavily framed kitchen chair. Her right elbow was resting on the same deal table. There were many people in the room, one or two moving about, but most of them had seated themselves on the settle or along the walls on chairs like her own. The men were blackfaced with white eyes; sweaty, too, their shirts open at the collar: the fire must have been got under. But it was their strange silence she noticed most, that and the way they were staring at her.

Mary came to her with a bowl of milk and said with unexpected kindness:

"You must drink it up; you're weak with the hunger."

She answered:

"Is there great damage done abroad?"

"There is; we're broke out; we're ruined. But don't be thinking about that."

"God knows 'twasn't I put the flame to it."

"Drink it up; drink the milk."

She drank it all. As she put the bowl on the table she said:

"You don't believe me? But 'tis true. That's what brought me in, to tell you so."

She saw Mary hesitate; then she heard:

"And you don't know who done it maybe?"

The voice was hard, although not much louder than breath. In the same whisper she answered again:

"God knows I don't know who done it."

The servant roughly gathered the bowl from the table, and as she turned from the dresser snappishly flung at her:

"Your brother's pipe, there 'tis there on the table."

A very old short-stemmed pipe, black as bogoak, lay in the centre of the white-scoured table—that and nothing else. She put out her hand and drew it to her. She knew every eye in the silent room was on her. She fondled it in her fist: he must have left it behind him when he was driven away in the cart to the poorhouse; 'twas nice of them to have kept it for her. She was surprised.

But then she noticed Mary still staring at her, saw her approach, again hesitatingly, and heard her speak, saying:

"And Michael himself, he's in the room below, and God have mercy on him."

By the room below she meant the room that opened from the kitchen at the far end of it. Margaret twisted her head to see it; she saw a glimmer of quiet candlelight in it. She stood up with indignant strength: one or two others stood up also, as if they could not help it, almost as if they would stop her. With firmness she went towards the glimmer, filled the doorway for a moment, against the light, and turned to the left into the lighted room, leaving silence behind her.

Only for the four candles alight on the white-clothed table she could see nothing, for only a tiny window lit the room. In the corner farthest from it she caught a glimpse of a bed: she saw her brother's face: with its eyes steadily shut it seemed to await in stillness her judgment. There had been some attempt made to lay him out decently. With a wild cry she flung herself on her knees by the bedside and began to call upon his name, in light tones, in whispers, commandingly, coaxingly, but always hurriedly: "Michael! Michael! Michael! Michael!" Between her clasped hands she held the pipe he had coloured so well. In the room she had left, a low whispering began and went from one to another, their heads drawing closer and closer.

III

The sheds at that time were, of course, all built of stone and heavily thatched with straw. The timbers used in them were

clumsy and weighty. The fire had had much to feed upon:
it had left them all quite roofless, only that here and there a
charred rafter or beam showed meagrely against the sky.
The hayrick was gone, too; a low pile of shining, steaming,
smoking blackness lay where it had been built up. The winter's supply of turf was gone as well: it had glowed like a furnace, the heat from it filling the whole haggard even against
the wind. The labourer had kept his head; he had thought
at once of freeing the animals—the plough horse, the milkers. But it was much later than that that he came on Michael;
it was in the shed he had freed the cattle from he found him:
he was only just within the door of it; lying at ease, his back
against the wall, his right hand stretched beside him, and
his pipe almost within reach of it: it had slipped from the
hand as sleep, or death, relaxed its hold. The fire, which
seemed to have started at his very feet, had not touched him.
The wind had driven it from him.

Clouds of smoke still volleyed away from the blackened
heaps of hay and straw: little rills of flame would start up
suddenly and run blindly along them for a few inches or a
few feet and die swiftly and brilliantly in the wind that had
caused them. Burnt wisps and flakes and tatters went still
flying busily across the fields like withered leaves, a continuing whirl. The air was acrid and choking; and everywhere the ground was in a puddle from the water that had
been flung, uselessly enough, upon the burning debris. Between the running water, the flying smuts, the smoke, the
smell, there was an active misery where at dawning had been
the homely comfort of a well-kept haggard into which the
harvest and the fuel had both been gathered against the winter. And that selfsame misery had got into the house as well.
Most of those who had helped were now quitting the place
to be in time for the evening milking in their own stalls; but
others, women and men and boys, some from quite distant
nooks of the parish, were still constantly arriving, for the

strangeness of the sudden calamity was being told of on every road. Many of these had never entered the house at all, only hung about in groups after exploring the sheds and the haggard. Some of them did find their way in, and over and over again the woman of the house had to go through the whole story from the beginning; until she had become irritable with weariness. This thing and that thing they would propose, but she would put them off, saying it was for the man of the house to settle matters like that.

Meanwhile the candles burned steadily in the lower room, the mourner sitting beyond them, taking not the least notice of such of the visitors as would enter and, falling on their knees by the bed, remain for a few minutes silent in prayer. Sometimes she herself would fall once again into a fit of crying; but since Mary had told her how they had found her brother, patience seemed to be more and more winning upon her passion. Of that those in the other room, the living room, were glad: surely, they thought, what the man of the house was to return to was bad enough without having such moanings as hers in his ears while he sat at his meal after his day's hard trafficking.

With darkness up rose the harvest moon right opposite the door of the house; it had to surmount a long-stretching ridge of rock, so that, when it appeared, its face was hard and bright, with mellowness shed quite away from it. It showed up everything sharply, callously. And the wind had fallen.

The very way the master sat upon the horse, bent forward, the way he kept it stepping briskly, forcing it, for clearly it was exhausted, told the gathered groups that he had been informed of the trouble. They saw that he had his mind made up not to stop in the yard to examine what damage had been done; not more than a glance he gave to the roofless sheds as he rounded the gable of the house. Where he was to tie up the animal they didn't know, but he soon returned on foot, an oldish man earnestly speaking up into his face, the master answering roughly: "I know. I know."

He was inclined to sit straightway at the meal prepared for him, but his wife reasoned with him in a low voice: things were bad enough without giving it to say that he wouldn't kneel by the bed of their old faithful servant. So he, too, went into the room and knelt by the feet of the dead man. Margaret took no more notice of him than of the others, though indeed the perfect stillness, the hush, that fell upon the whole place as he knelt might have told her enough. Then he withdrew, quietly, drawing the door of the room out behind him as he did so. He sat to the table, the silence almost as deep as before. His brows were bent, his expression surly, as he took an egg cup in his hand to break the shell. He didn't notice, but everyone else in the room did, that the door of the death-chamber began to turn silently on its hinges. They saw Margaret appear; they thought she would come forth; but no; she simply remained between the two rooms, her back against the jamb of the door; they could see her outline against the light of the candles within, her eager face directed in towards her brother. As if she had been, in her mind, speaking to him for a long time, they heard her voice glide into rising speech: they all hung forward to see and to hear; but the man of the house never moved, only bent more over the table, his left shoulder raised a little between himself and the voice: he would not hear it, would not give it his attention. But the words she uttered live on, at least in part, in those quiet homes to this very day:

"Surely, Michael, it was strange to have you crossing the stepping-stones coming from the south, making no noise in the darkness, and I to be crossing the stepping-stones coming from the north, as if someone I was afraid of was driving me on: you crossing the Lee of the white flowers and I crossing the Flesk of the white stones. Surely, Michael, it was strange, and strange enough, to have you secretly undoing these gates and entering this haggard from the south, and I

without a sound stealing into it from the north. Why didn't
you stretch your stick from you, and you would have touched
me with the tip of it and you could say: Who is that? And
why didn't I give a little cough out of me for you to hear?
But the darkness was against us—that was it. It was kind
for you to feel your way to the homely beasts and make your
bed beside them. In the sheds you had a comfortable house
for yourself; but I had no luck at all, for the roads of the
world had taught me hardness and courage, and so 'twas the
threshold I made for; but the door was closed and the windows dark: my hearthstone was the cold flagstone outside,
my knees to my chin and my cloak all over me. I was like a
pedlar's bundle fallen from a cart that no one would notice
until the daylight came: wasn't that the cold shelter I had
the live-long night, and you with the warm beasts beside
you shaking the timbers of the stalls in their sleeping. And
now 'tis you are the cold one."

Here, the people have handed down, she made a long
pause; and the silence grew worse and worse to bear. Then
she went on:

"Michael Cumeen, you were no scatterer; you did not lin-
ger in public-houses nor in gaming houses. You did not spend
your money foolishly; and I won't know what to answer
when I am asked where is the fortune your brother left you,
for a little black pipe without even a fill of tobacco in it is no
answer at all.

"Ah, little black pipe in the heel of my fist, 'twas from you
the little sparkeen fell out, and if the wind stirred it along
like a bright young corncrake in the stubble, that was the
will of God, for you were fast in your sleep and wasn't listening at all to the beasts rattling the timbers of the stalls in the
uneasiness. And so it was appointed for you to die beside the
cattle you tended so well, and not among the paupers of the
south. God be kind to you for you were no scatterer at all.
You were all for saving. The people will understand, they'll

say how you saved for others and not for your own; and I will answer them and say: you have the right of it: he gathered into the sheds he built up for them, he gathered into them until they were cracking and bursting. If you don't believe me, I'll say, go up to them and see; and God will lift up the moon for you to see by like a lamp. And 'tis good-bye to you now, Michael; for myself, too, would like to see the riches you gathered into the sheds in fifty years. With my little black pipe in the heel of my fist I'll point them out to all the parish who are gathering to this place! They won't be without something to tell their children and their children's children!"

With that she bent her head to her brother and said her prayer; and quietly turned to leave; but the man of the house leaped up from the table crying out "Stop! Stop!" His wife, however, and all those who were present, gathered about him and prevailed on him to sit again. By that time Margaret had gone. She didn't bother, they say, to view the broken sheds in the moonlight, or to point them out, only went her way silently, the hushed groups drawing back for her to pass. Not a soul followed her; they were afraid. Nor can one of their children's children say where it was appointed for her to die when her own time was come. But her words live on; and the Houlihans live on also, or rather their children's children.

On the Heights

....

I

A STRANGER handed in a little slip of paper at the door of the farmhouse in Acharas where I had been hiding for several weeks: within ten minutes of receiving it I was on my bicycle, was flying at break-neck speed down mountainy bohereens, one after another, crossing through watercourses without dismounting, and skimming the sharp corners of boulders by half inches or less. And yet I was all but caught! Only for their hooting, as their motor swerved from the main road, I had ridden into their arms. I caught that hoot! hoot! and flung from my path by very instinct; slapdash in among the rocks and furze I went, went as far as I could, then threw myself off on the heather, and breathing like a swimmer after a long swim against time, could do nothing but wait, helpless. Puffing and panting on my knees, I could see them between the rocks: with frowning determination they were putting their heavy military motor at the hill, and I recognised the sergeant in charge. "Mullery!" I gasped, and grabbed my handlebar again by instinct. If I fell into Mullery's hands, it meant five years: he was a man that would swear anything. When they had gone by, I mounted again, and swept into Gougane Barra by the back road, and was just making on for Keimaneigh when something spoke in my ear—perhaps it was the old Gaelic saints who lie there at rest—" They will have set a watch in Keimaneigh: take the

mountains." And so, instead of taking the comfortable if heavy road through the Pass of Keimaneigh, I made straight for Coomroe, facing the great walls of rock that enclose that most impressive of mountain glens. I have never heard that any other mortal ever pushed a bicycle up the one thousand eight hundred feet of jagged rock that hangs above the inches there; but I did it, how I do not know, unless it was the vision of that dogged face in the motor car that kept me ever pushing on and on and up and up.

As I shoved, dragged, slided, lifted my wheels up the rocks, the sweat ran freely and warmly down my back and limbs. I gave it no thought, I felt no weariness. But when I reached the summit and expected to see the sun again, a cold sea wind struck me, refreshed me, and then, suddenly, chilled me; and up before me rose a wall of white mist. I looked for the mountain-peaks that used to guide me there, but none were visible in the cloud. Feeling it all around me, licking and stroking me, and remembering how warm it had been in the coom, I knew I was making into a night of rain; and there are no wetter hills in the whole of Munster. As I went forward I tried to recollect the whereabouts of the nearest house in those forlorn uplands, but all my landmarks were blotted out. I came suddenly on a close-huddled flock of black-faced mountainy sheep; they looked at me and scampered off into the mists with timid cries; they, too, seemed to be waiting for the rain. I felt lonelier than before. The pursuit was over and done with—years ago, it appeared. I thought of it no more. Could I make the Coomahola river before night-fall, was the only question that would rise up in my mind, as I pushed my bicycle now over the shale and then through growths of fragrant bog-myrtle. And it would come into my mind, too, that though I was making forward with fair speed I was doing no good, for I did not know where I was going. Yet somehow I feared to stop. I stumbled on and on, till suddenly I saw beside me a flat table of rock, about two feet high, as perfectly shaped as if stonecutters had worked at it. Before I had willed it, it seemed, I was sitting on it with a sense of delicious ease. "I will think out exactly where I am and where I will go," I said, comforting myself with a pretence of will power that I knew well was but a pretence. Then down came the rain, slanting from the south-west.

II

I bowed my head to it in sheer hopelessness—and that action it was that saved me. Beneath my eyes I saw certain light marks on the ground, not wheel marks—they were not more than two feet six apart, and besides they were not cut into the ground. I was instantly following them. I knew what they were. They were the marks of a "tray," as the peasants of that place call it both in Irish and English—a sort of light sleigh on which they bring down the cut turf from places in the uplands that are too steep for horse and cart. These marks meant a house, sooner or later. With the greatest care I kept to them. And soon I began to come on other signs of human ways and strivings—a cairn of stones, a first effort at a clearance, then a crazy sort of boundary fence, long abandoned to its own will, then at last two forked stakes in the ground, a young ash sapling laid across them, closing a gap. I blessed the human touch: the pious hands of husbandry had made it! Then I struck the path.

The night thickened, and the rain thickened; but now with the path beneath my feet, all broken shale it was, I did not mind. I thought I might leave my bicycle there until I had found the house, which I knew to be somewhere in the darkness. I laid it in the dripping heather and made more swiftly on. (I recovered it next day, clean as a new pin.) A waft of turf smoke struck me. I breathed it in with wide nostrils. My spirits rose, I could shout out. Then in a pit of darkness beneath me to the right I saw the tiny little eye of a lamplit window, warm-coloured, and looking as if its kindly gleam had been peering out that way on the hills for thousands and thousands of years, so steady it was. I used no caution. I made for it through the blackness, and lost the path. I found myself stumbling down the side of a little ravine—I splashed through a leaping stream, I almost fell upon the door. I banged it with my fist. I heard movement within, a collie whined, voices whispered. I could not wait. I banged again, and the rain pelted my warm wrist. I caught the latch and shook the door. "Open! Open!" I cried. Within, I heard the bolts being withdrawn.

A low-toned, uncertain voice spoke in my face:—

"Who are you? What is it you want? Come in. You're all wet."

A dull-looking, middle-aged man and his wife, a soft-featured, kindly creature, drew back from me, and continued to stare at me; I felt annoyed at their doubtful reception; there was no heartiness in it.

"I'm wet all right," I said, trying to speak calmly; but then I added with a bitterness I could not help, "there are more than me on the hills these times, and better than me."

By these words I would give them to understand why I was on the hills.

The man's jaw fell; he looked at his wife; they stared at me helplessly, even more stupidly than before, I thought, and more frigidly. He came one step towards me and whispered:—

"Maybe you'd speak low? Maybe you would?"

What did he mean?

"Draw up to the fire; take your coat off," the woman said, handing me a towel to wipe my face.

"Why should I speak low? Is there anyone sick?" I said, looking at the poor staring creature that was man of the house.

"No, no; there's no one sick, thanks be to God; glory be to His Holy Name!"

He was smiling at me in an indeterminate sort of way, his jaw hanging. He was a weak-mouthed man, I could see. He went doddering away. His wife pointed to the door in the partition at the end of the room.

"The old man, his father—he's asleep within, and he's noisy if anyone wakes him."

That then was why I should speak low. I understood. I had met such old men before—Lears, but Lears who get the best of the bargain, maintaining their rights of property to the very day that they have to step into the grave. We found ourselves speaking in whispers, all three of us, I trying to explain how I found the track to their lonely door and they wondering how I had missed the wider track across the hills. After all, they were a good hearted couple, and could enjoy a chat—if one carried it on in whispers.

The man raised his head suddenly: we all listened. The winds were coming up from Bantry Bay, they were roaring upon the roof. As we listened, in flew the door with a crash, the fire was scattered on the hearth, the sheep dog sprang from his sleep, planted his legs and howled at the storm. We all flung ourselves on the door. In the sudden tumult I forgot myself. As we got the door to I shouted with vast enjoyment:—

"There! there! stay outside now—with Sergeant Mullery," I added under my breath.

"Hush! hush! sir; lave ye."

Both man and wife were terrified, it seemed. They were looking towards the end of the room.

I put my hand to my mouth, hunching my shoulders, and turning like them towards the unseen sleeper—how we leap at moments back into our childhood! But too late, too late. Three dreadful blows were struck on that partition towards which we were all looking, and an aged but vigorous and indignant voice cried out above the storm in ringing Irish:—

"Am I to be kept always in the dark? Ever and always!

Look at me, and I for the last hour killed with listening to your foolery—and dogs—and giggling—and the stranger's voice stunning me; and 'tisn't worth your while, Shawn, to come in with a little word."

Man and wife were trying to smile at me; but I could see that they were used to getting the worse of it. They did not know what was best to do.

"I'll answer him," I said. They clutched me.

"No, no," they were whispering warmly in my face; "no, sir; no sir."

I cried out in Irish as ringing as his own:—

"You'd drive a stranger from your door, this night?" Half in jest, half in earnest, I spoke the words. The winds were roaring with a great voice; I could hear the cataracts pouring.

" 'Tis no decent person would be travelling the hills this night," I was answered, and there was suspicion and challenge in the tones.

"There's a more decent person on your floor this night," I answered back, and in spite of myself my voice was hard and rough, "a more decent person than ever walked this hungry land since St. Finnbarr left it, travelling to the east."

"Left it and blessed it," the voice answered me in triumph.

"I doubt it," I answered, and my anger was gone; and there came swiftly over me a joyousness to think of the two of us shouting at each other there in that lonely land with the roaring storm outside, grandest of orchestras.

"I doubt it," I cried, in a great voice.

"He did," he answered.

"I doubt it."

" 'Tis well known; the authors say so!"

My heart opened to him! How often I had heard that or similar phrases from his like! "*Se adeir na h-ughdair . . .*"

"If he did, ye ought to remember it, and not drive a stranger from. . . ."

"There's no one doing the like; but haven't I the right to complain if my son will not tell me who 'tis comes in or goes out? Come in to me, Shawn, and let you make the stranger his meal, Nora."

Shawn went into him, having first looked despairingly at his wife, who smiled back encouragingly. I felt I had not fathomed any one of the three of them.

"He'll be in his sleep in a moment," she said to me in a whisper. "You gave him his answer." She was more courageous than the man.

III

I made free with the big teapot of black tea she made me, and with the lovely bread, laughing to myself and yet wondering. After a while Shawn returned to us on tiptoe from the old man's room, and, silenced, we could hear the deep and vigorous breathing of his father.

I began telling them of the detestable war bread the people in the cities and towns had to eat, and of the great scarcity of everything among them; they sighed over them, the poor creatures! And so the night passed. I began to wonder why they did not suggest retiring, for it was now near midnight. I began to yawn involuntarily, and to measure the settle with my eyes. I had often slept on one. They were again confused. At last the man, who was certainly an extraordinarily gentle creature, touched my sleeve shyly and said: "The only place we have for you to sleep in is with himself," he nodded towards the partition. I was just about to say, "What about the settle?" when I thought suddenly that there were but the two rooms in the house; I glanced about and saw that the press on which the candle was lighting was of course a folded-up bedstead. Yet I didn't answer: I did not relish the thought of sleeping with a person I had just quarrelled with.

"You could slip in—quietly. He sleeps sound."

I smiled at him.

"Go in," I said, throwing myself erect, "and tell him the police and the soldiers are on my track, and see what he'll say?"

I felt sure that anyone who kept the "authors" in his thoughts would not refuse a corner of his bed to a rapparee. I was surprised how they took my words! Had they not known it?

"No, no," they both cried warmly at me; "not that way at all," the man moved about the flags in trouble.

" 'Tis better say no word about the soldiers or police at all," the wife urged; "only that 'tis how a tourist is after losing his way in the fogs, a tourist was fishing in Loch Fada. Go on, Shawn, and tell him that; 'tis a story will do no one any harm."

I consented, and Shawn went very timidly into his father's presence. We listened; yet there was no noise between them, no squabbling at all. He came out gesturing that the way was clear. About midnight I stepped very carefully over the old man's rather bulky figure, to take my share of the huge old bed.

"Out the candle," he growled at me. Timidly enough I mumbled an apology, and did so. Outside, the winds shrieked among the upland gullies and the waters fell in them.

IV

I awoke with some dim feeling of annoyance. It was pitch dark and the storm was still roaring, but near by was an unceasing whisper, a sharp hissing of breath between teeth and lips: the old man, hunched up in the bed, was praying. I dozed off again, and again I woke, and the hissing was still going on beside me. He was, I suspected, carrying out a practice of fifty or sixty years' standing. To the roaring winds outside he was deaf: he knew their voices better than I. I was listening to them, to him, thankful for the nest of warmth and peace I found myself in. I would occasionally hear the rattle of his beads, and from the sound could guess at their huge size. Dozing again, I heard him gather them up; and then I am quite clear I heard the words, " . . . and for the souls of all the men they put to death in Dublin!" His voice fell to a whisper, and a vigorous "Amen!" finished his prayers, as with a clasp. He shrugged the clothes up about his shoulders, groped under the pillow, and settled himself to sleep. A sudden rush of thought and feeling swept over me. "The souls of all the men they put to death in Dublin," I repeated, and I thought of this lonely old man praying for them in this unknown cabin on the uplands. In the phrase of the people, I was glorified to think of it.

Yet presently I fell to wondering why his son and his son's wife had implored me not to tell him that I was a hunted man on the hills. I could not understand it.

V

I awoke in the bright morning to find the old man's fingers touching and feeling my brow with great gentleness. He started when my eyes glared up at him. It was then I saw him for the first time with any distinctness. He had a fringe of white, wool-white whiskers in under his shaven chin; he looked like a shepherd in an old play or in a picture; but there was a keenness and a sharpness about the brow—an alertness that made one forget this first thought of him. Seeing how he had started, I greeted him in good Irish. He smiled at me:—

"You're no tourist was fishing Loch Fada," he said, knowingly. I listened a moment; there was no stir in the room outside. I felt sure they had not yet risen, had not yet been speaking to him. The sun was bathing the hills, a robin was singing. Even in the little darksome cabin there was an air of freshness and gladness.

"What am I, then?" I said.

"You're no tourist," he said again, with the same wise and, I thought, encouraging smile.

"But what am I?"

"I'll tell you: you're one of them!" He gave me a slow, antique wink; it was like a gesture. "I was one of them myself and I young," he added. He flung up his head.

"It wasn't I told you I was a tourist."

"No, 'twas himself. But you, 'twas yourself, and no one else, told me—told me what I know. Brother," he said, using the familiar word among the Gaels, "you were dreaming . . . powerful dreams!" What wild foolery had I been crying out in my sleep! His eyes were full of vision—my dreams!

" 'Twill come to pass," he said, "the authors foretold it." I had no reply, except to stare at him, his face aglow, bending upon mine.

"But isn't this a pitiful thing," he grew mournful above me, "that man outside, that son of mine—he's a thing without courage, he's like a sheep after being worried by the dogs, he is that! He'd be afraid to hang a bit of green on the door, or to keep a gun in the house. I'm sick and tired of him. But look, forgive me the welcome I gave you: these times there do be men in plain clothes going from house to house, innocent-looking slobs of men, gathering up information, and that pair outside, I must be watching them. 'Tisn't too much I'd tell them." He repeated that solemn wink of his.

I left him still in his bed, and I sat at breakfast with the two others.

"You got on all right with himself?"

"I did, I did, then."

"He's a bit cross sometimes; he was a Fenian in the old days."

"He told me so."

They looked sharply at me. They were wondering how much he had told me. And in that state of mind I left them.

The Aherns

··

I

BECAUSE I knew no house in that country (we had not then opened it up; now we have no less than three strong companies of Volunteers there—fine fellows), I took my chance in the little hotel. It was the usual kind of hotel one finds in a place that has neither charm nor business of its own—just a public-house, with a few stuffy little bedrooms. For whole months at a time it would doubtless forget that it was a hotel at all. Then some old-time angler would alight on it, or a commercial traveller, thinking he had discovered a virgin land and would work it, or some sort of official from Dublin. For some weeks after the passage of one of these it would still wear somehow the flaunt of a hotel, but mostly it was just a public-house by the side of a road in a grazing district, somnolent in the summer and almost forgotten in the winter—shuttered the whole day long, its door closed out.

Except for a middle-aged man named Harley—an angler, with a pursed-out, gloomy, silent mouth, I had the house to myself. I was in bed before he had come down from the lake in the hills: I hoped to be far on my road before he would rise in the morning, and I therefore saw no use in deepening our half-hour's acquaintanceship. I remember I did hear him come in, I did hear the corks popping in the silent night. But I had fallen again to sleep when, all confused for a moment, I heard the sudden rush of a motor. Its speed was so great that I felt sure of its passing when, without a voice in the night, I heard it swerve towards the house and stop up, its stifled energy setting my room quivering. Then there were voices enough, quick, low, hard, certain of themselves. I heard the rattle of guns, footsteps noisily making up the stairs, and the publican's voice wailing out, "It's not fair of ye, gentlemen, it's not fair at all." I was had! I felt a sort of disgust, of sickness; the swiftness of the capture, the ease of it, staggered me. I had not even left my bed; I had not even thought of flight.

They were tapping, peremptorily, at poor Harley's door. They were turning the handle, walking in to him—bayonets and all! They were now at my door. It was flung in, a flash of light sweeping walls and ceiling.

In my sleep, my left elbow raised itself to keep out the dazzle of their lanterns, and I grumbled thickly. Voices were whispering. I knew the landlord pushed them aside. "Gentlemen, gentlemen, can't ye see he's not the man ye're after."

I growled again, puffing out my lips. "You mustn't speak," I heard. It was the District Inspector's voice, I could tell that.

" 'Twas four to one, damn and blast your soul," I rapped out, up in their very faces.

"Can't ye see? 'Tis a farmer's son he is, was at the Junction —where else? and lost his money."

They shook me.

"Your name, what's your name?"

"It has nothing to do with it—you'll hand over the money or . . ." and without putting a tooth in them I flung a handful of terrible words up in their very mouths.

"By damn," said the landlord, " 'tis how he won; 'twas whiskey he was drinking, too, all I had." He chuckled. I felt him by me.

"Waking or sleeping, 'twould be all the same; 'tis little ye'd get from him—wake up, sonny," he urged. But he gave my arm a sharp little nip the moment he said it. I was too drunk to wake, my head went from side to side on the pillow, like a child's head of a hot summer's night. They were whispering. "Wake up, sonny," he said again. I could hear Harley's voice timidly calling him. "I'm coming, I'm coming, sir." He nipped my arm again.

I felt him going. What would happen next? "I don't believe 'tis him," I heard. I raised at once a long rigmarole; there was neither sense nor meaning in it, but I kept it up; and I would repeat the one sentence six times running without the slightest pause at the endings. And while I was in it —that outburst of speech—I felt the room grow calm and cool and silent around me. They had stolen away.

After all, it was not I that they were seeking. It was Killeenan; they had tracked him right from Dublin to this countryside and then lost him, from their very hands, as it were. But there was a voice among those whisperers around my bed, and I had had dealings with that voice already; I had heard it giving evidence against me at a courtmartial in Cork; it had got me condemned to three years' imprisonment—not one month of which I had served. Sergeant Naylor would, I think, be quite content with me as a capture that rich night in autumn: I should, anyhow, be far better than no one.

II

A curious thing happened when they were gone. I was sitting up in the bed, listening to their car getting off into the hills like a swift wind, when the landlord slipped into my room, softly turning the lock on the door behind him. As quietly again, he lit the candle, drew the one chair to my bed and sat on it, looking at me with a strange smile. In this deliberation I could see he was trying to hide his high-strung nervousness.

"Do you know me?" I asked him.

"No," he said; "but I knew what you were the moment you came in the door."

I was surprised; he had not by the slightest look or word let me understand that he knew my business.

"How did you know what I was?"

He smiled again, lifted himself, and gave his head the slightest little toss. I knew it at once; but must own that I had never observed it till then. Our lads use it at the courts-martial when, asked if they have anything to say, they reply, as in a formula, "I want to say that I haven't a dog's respect for this court or its findings." I had never observed it till then, as I say, and I was quite unaware that it could be observed in me in my ordinary moments—observed, moreover, by a country publican! He was smiling with a certain shyness in his eyes. I held my hand out to him.

"I'm thankful to you," I said.

"Didn't we do it well, better than if we were after planning it out beforehand?" His look was all eagerness.

"Far better," was all I could say.

"I don't know how I did it. I was never any use at deceiving people, let alone the likes of them; something kept me up. . . ." His voice suddenly weakened, his fingers went trailing weakly across his forehead. I saw sweat standing on it. He was turning white. I leaped from the bed.

"Hold up! 'Tis nothing, 'tis nothing."

He hadn't a word in him. I thought there might be some whiskey in Harley's room. I made for it, candle in hand. He had just got into bed for the second time. I laid my hand on a little flask. "The old man is not well; he's after fainting. They frightened him."

To give him his due he wanted to come with me; but I would not allow him.

"I'm getting old, I suppose," said the publican, when the weakness had passed. "A man should be able to stand more than that—these times," he added, with that quaint shy smile of his.

I put my landlord to bed—(there was no one else in the

house but the three of us)—and I left him very proud and happy at having saved me from my enemies.

" 'Twould be frightful if they nabbed you under my roof," he said.

III

I am sure I would have slept all right if it were not for this second disturbance. I remained sitting up in my bed, smoking cigarette after cigarette; and it came to me, I do not know how, that Sergeant Naylor would recollect having seen my face before, might even recollect when and where; and in two minutes I was dressing myself with quick fingers.

I slipped silently down the stairs, and I remember noticing the stuffy smell in the shop, and wondering how it could be as stuffy as that in such an open, windy country. I slipped the bolts—there were four of them—turned the key in the lock, and very quietly rolled my bicycle from the door in the stillness of the misty dawn. I crept softly forward. Down came the gable window.

"Young man, I say, young man, where are you going?"

"Sh!—sh!" I breathed at him, " 'tis better for me to go. They'll come back." I watched his white hair sticking out in tufts around his head. There was an innocence in his look that made me think of a woman's face. The world and its hard wisdom, for some reason, had passed him by.

"But you'll have something before you'll start?"

"No, no; 'tis better not. I know where to go. I'll have a good breakfast, I'll warrant you."

"You will, you will." These were not the words he would say, I felt.

"You'll be welcome here any time, night or day. Ye're suffering ye'r own share, running like the poor hare and the dogs upon ye," he immediately added.

The chilly dawn was around me and its great stillness.

"There are others suffering more—the men in English

prisons," I answered; and, having said it, I was just mounting when two lines of Sean Clarach's came into my mind, and I flung up my head and chanted them to the white old head in the window:—

> *"Is iomdha mac dilis dibeartha uaim,*
> *Is a Chriost, nach truagh me 'na n-easbaidhe"*—

"The same old story?" I said, with a sudden bitterness, still speaking in Irish.

"I don't understand ye," he said, in a sort of wail, "but it's great to hear ye speaking that language; it reminds me of them that's gone—great men! great men!"

I waved a hand, and left him there, staring after me in the silent morning.

IV

About ten miles off was a country I knew when a boy, I had often spent vacations in it. As I rode and rode, Sean Clarach's earnest words gradually went from my mind, and the beautiful autumn morning began to wrap me about with quiet pleasure. And I began to think of the farmer's son I had known in the old days in this place towards which I was making: we had fished its streams together for long days, and ridden the one horse to the little town on messages. And the thought of him, so gentle he always was, fitted into my mood, and still further quieted it, enriched it, too—those old days had been so sweet and homely, and the later days so full of anxiety and rush and uncertainty. I swept round a corner which was shadowy with trees, and then dismounted; nothing else could I have done; there on the hillside before me was my friend's house—Gregory Ahern's house.

I told myself he must now be a man, but I could picture him only as a boy. These were *our* fields. I looked all over them, one after another. As with all Ireland the place had improved very much—sheds had been added, barns had begun to cluster about the house, and a screen of larch had been planted against the north-east. It was so prosperous-looking that I had some slight fear that it might have passed into other hands. At last, I wheeled my bicycle up the bohereen and through the farmyard. The house door was open. An old man greeted me: an oblique rectangle of sharp sunlight fell on the floor, reaching to his feet.

" 'Tis," he said; "you're at the right house."

"And you," I said, "are Humphrey Ahern."

"The same," he said, cautiously.

"You don't know me?"

He raised his eyes and kept them fixed on me.

"Pardon me," he said, with an easy courtesy that brought vividly back to me the boy Gregory I had known in the old days; there was something in him that, even then, I used to wonder at, not able to name it.

"Pardon me," he blinked at me, "the rheumatism has me destroyed. I can't rise, and I cannot see with the sun." He made an effort to rise.

"It's fifteen years since I was last in this place," I said, coming close to him, "your son, Gregory, would know me."

"If he knew you then, he won't deny you now." I thought there was a touch of meaning in his words: had I been tossing my head in the air, I wondered?

"Gregory, and all of them, are in the sheds with the cows; they'll be here in a moment; rest yourself."

V

The womenfolk came in first. They had no difficulty in recalling me: they asked after my people. Then Gregory came —my old friend—only now six feet in height, big of bone, keen-eyed, a little jerky in movement. His voice was indistinct, his whole bearing had that excessive gentleness that is so common in Munster. His diffidence almost prevented speech. After some time:—

"I read your book," he said. "I have it inside," he nodded towards the little parlour.

I was surprised. My little book of poems had not, I had very good reason to know, voyaged far beyond my friends in Dublin.

"And you were in the Rising, and in Frongoch; I was going to write to you. . . . I didn't. . . ."

He glanced shyly at me: his eyes fell. I had reddened a little. The fact is I had never thought of him for years and years! His people were staring at me. They evidently had as yet never met anyone who had gone through that terrible week in Dublin or slept in prisons. And he, surely, had kept all this to himself. He had enshrined me! I could see it; and I stumbled in my speech, as a consequence, fearing that the least hint of the Dublin literary man or the hero of many prisons would break from me. I tried to keep my head steady as one does for a photographer. His people had become more than polite: the old man was examining me with steady eyes and pursed lips, thinking his thoughts.

At our meal of home-made cake, eggs and tea, with great shyness Gregory said: "I read an article you wrote in 'The Rebel'; it was called 'When the gods arrive, the half-gods go' —I thought it good—perhaps I have no right——" I checked him. Other articles, too, wayside things, he recalled; he had treasured them for my sake. I feared he would quote them, repeat them!

"You should have written to me," I said.

"Gregory isn't the boy to do a thing like that," his aunt broke in, smiling with quiet eyes. He gave a little shrug, and stood upright, staring through the open door.

I couldn't place him, my mind couldn't cover his with any confidence; I had met that type of Munsterman before, had discovered unexpected depths in them—a grit that is not blatant. It has often failed us of the Volunteers to make drill sergeants out of them; but they may keep a whole country-side up to the mark. They go to America, to England, to Glasgow and keep labour politics red hot! I tremble before them. And Gregory was, I could see, even among the type quite exceptional: his own people had even noticed it. I was not at ease, the more so on account of that head-toss the publican had discovered in me. I knew I had lately developed, in my flying from place to place, from company to company, something of the soldier of fortune—indeed we, all of us, put on the soldier of fortune a little too often, sometimes as a mask, sometimes for the sport of the thing. I would redden with shame if now the least hint of that hail-fellow-well-met boisterousness came to the top. Gregory's type shrink before such loudness, abashed, and yet deeply scornful. And perhaps it was to avoid any such display that I began to speak of my escape from the District Inspector—an incident where my part was not heroic. I stopped suddenly—they were examining me with such earnest eyes. "Oh, but there was no danger, no danger at all. They wouldn't have shot me! At the worst it might have meant three years. . . ."

"But if you resisted?"

"But I wouldn't——"

" 'Tis the publican we're thinking of," said Gregory's father.

"How?" I said.

"He didn't betray you?"

I was glad to speak of the publican's part, of how he had helped me, as with the surety of instinct. I told of my leaving him, of my thankfulness. They lifted up, looking at one another.

"He's an uncle of Gregory's," the old man shook his head at his son.

"Your brother?" I said.

"The same," he replied quietly.

" 'Tis in the blood," I whispered, under my breath.

The next moment I was sorry I had told them all this. I was now not only a man on his keeping, but one almost within the clutches of his pursuers. Already I could see them glancing through the windows: a labouring boy, who had been listening, rose up and casually strolled through the door to the gate of the farmyard, stood there a moment looking east, looking west, as if sniffing the air. Coming back he threw himself along the settle. "He's another Ahern," I said to myself.

Gregory himself had fallen into an unbroken silence. Once or twice I caught him glancing at me, and I would question myself whether I had bragged or spoken cheaply or tossed my head. How much easier it is to face the hot little eyes of the martinets who preside at the courtsmartial than it is to meet those questioning eyes where admiration wrestles with old love!

VI

I slept with Gregory that night. Even when we were alone, I sitting on his bed, he smoking the cigarette I had given him, I couldn't win him from his reserve. I got in first. His voice changing a little, he jerked out: "Are you sure there's no danger? Couldn't we mount guard? Jack and myself; 'twould be only a couple of hours each. He'll be glad to do so; I know him."

I laughed.

"You need to knock about a bit."

"Everyone says that," he jerked his head, half-piteously, half-humorously.

I do not know how many hours I had slept when I awoke quietly from a pleasant sleep. As one will in a strange room, I had to look for the window. There, with a start, I saw Gregory with his head thrust out into the air!

"Gregory! For the love of heaven, what are you doing there?"

"Nothing, nothing, I couldn't sleep. I fancied I heard people prowling."

"Have sense, boy, have sense!"

"Everything is quiet," he said, coming from the window.

"I declare," I said, " 'tis I will have to mount guard over you."

"I really thought I heard something . . . only for that——"

"If you rise again I'll go out and sleep in the shed—I'd have more peace and quietness."

"But supposing you were caught here in our house."

"Lord! The Aherns would never recover from the shame of it!"

He laughed.

"We're not used to it."

"What?" I said.

"Having people like you with us—felons—rebels. . . . I suppose I'd make a bad soldier?"

A bad soldier! He was like a young colt that would tremble and dance about the field—but once in the race!

The next time I woke 'twas with the sweat standing on my brow. I was being hanged, but for all that they could not stifle my voice. Hundreds of them were there before me, their faces white and distorted with passion—moving, drawing close to me, vanishing. Everything was in movement; and it was my voice that had caused it. I was making a speech such as had never been made before on the scaffold—flinging out taunts to them that made them squirm and vanish from my eyes! And all the time I was being stifled. . . . When I awoke Gregory's long, and, truth to tell, strong and bony arm was fiercely around my neck. You might see a wooden horse so grasped in the arm of a sleeping child!

Disengaging his arm, though I did so with all gentleness, he almost awoke. "What! what!" he murmured, and then a crowd of little words ran from him. But he was fast in his sleep. I breathed easily: I could not bear that he should know he had gripped me like that. I do not know what he was dreaming of; but I am sure of one thing, however; whatever it was it was not he who was playing the leading part in it, making fine speeches, casting heroic scorn on his country's enemies.

.   .   .   .

Time has passed. Yes, he keeps that whole countryside *firm*. He has it in his grip. He will be dragged from his house some night and shot. Or he may, in the end, die in prison of a hunger strike. He will not fail, nor look a fool—the big things being come.

An Unfinished Symphony

●●●

I

I WOULD dare it—and my heart leaped and sang as soon as I had spoken. God knows, I was drained of spirit. If those young men of that countryside, those young Republicans, who were ready to dare all, to take five years in jail without making any defence, whose brothers had died that the infant Republic might be set up, who would die themselves to maintain it—if those young men I was finding flat, shallow, dull, commonplace! in myself was the fault, as I told myself ten times a day. Every morning now I arose unfit for the day's work (I was organising the Intelligence Department of the Republican Volunteer Army in that eastern part of County Cork), and during the actual conferences I would find my mind wandering, and I would find the men looking at me shrewdly, perplexed at my casual way of doing the thing; and yet I could not, try as I might, win back to my old energy; I had grown suddenly stale—that was all that was to be said.

And then suddenly, and by the merest chance, I heard that Eibhlin Ni Chartha, or Eileen MacCarthy, if you find it easier to remember that form of her name, was in Knockacashlawn, which is not very far from Mogeela, which is itself on the railway—that she would be there for some weeks with some relatives of hers, and that her coming there had already made a difference. A difference?—surely, surely! I had no doubt at all I would find a very efficient Cumann na mBan

in the place, ready for all emergencies; I would find them
learning Irish, learning First Aid, learning how to cook on
an open fire, above all, I would find them learning—Eibhlin
herself! Yes, I would go to her.

There would be no need to explain anything. Owing to my
way of living these few years past, running from place to
place, seldom daring to sleep at home, we had never "fixed
matters up," as people say, but I was confidently certain that
Eibhlin would become one day my wife, and this I knew that
she knew just as well as I. In the wells of her spirit I would
bathe. We would laugh, we would cycle, we would dance
the *rinnce fada* in the farm kitchens, we would play cards
with the labourers, we would borrow the farmers' hunters
and make the frosty roads ring beneath our hoofs, we would
go shooting in the bogs—we would climb the high hills, we
would surprise the simple people who were giving us so
large-heartedly of their stores, of their pity, of their love.
They would say: "Those Sinn Feiners—look how merry they
can be—and they not knowing the night they'll be flung
into prison, or maybe shot or hanged!" Then, after five days,
or eight, or ten, I would take up my work again, and push
ahead with it, rejoicing in those gifts of insight and tact that
God had given me. Yes, I would dare all and go to her.

II

This was the risk: the police, as I well knew, had still the
thought that I had never left the Mogeela district! I had
heard that even still the young men in those parts would
stroll lazily and sleepily from their fathers' houses of a morning—with little or nothing to do these wintry days—and find
a few policemen disappearing round a corner—policemen
who had been peeping in at their windows or listening at
their doors and shutters, seeking a strange accent, a strange
face, seeking my poor self! For me, then, there was risk, but
as I told myself, for the Republic there was greater risk in

my staying where I was, dawdling at the work instead of doing it. So could it be reasoned out, I said, my going to Knockacashlawn; but only little had reason to say to it: I was doing right in going there, reason or no reason. I knew, I felt deep down in me, that I was doing right!

And the first stage of my journey went well with me. I kept to the up-hill, down-hill, ancient, overgrown by-roads of the pack-horse centuries, some of them nowadays just tracks on a hillside; and I dashed into the railway station at just the right moment to fling myself into a carriage—I knew the lack of a ticket would make no difference—all the men on that part of the line were "ours." They knew me of old. "Thank God! Thank God!" I said, almost aloud, when I found the train moving nicely off, passing the stolid policemen, who, chin in air, quite efficiently surveyed us as we passed, catching sight, perhaps, of a young man, or at least of a large handkerchief wiping the sweaty face and brow of a young man in a third class carriage. Thank God, so much was over, and I had three-quarters of an hour before anything else could happen.

I found myself examining, rather with interest, two old maiden ladies, the only other human souls in the carriage, and I was surprised to find myself doing so; already I was being renewed; or else I could not have given myself up to this quiet contemplation of them. They were dainty old ladies, sisters to all seeming: the piece of purple ribbon in the furs of the one was flesh of the flesh of the piece of purple ribbon in the hat?—bonnet?—hat? of the other. In equal parts they had shared out their rather ample stock of old-fashioned jewellery—I could match one thing with another. Sisters, yet with a difference, as two blossoms on the one plant may differ. Their heads were turned from me, they were intent on the wintry landscape passing by, so intent that I knew that everyone of all their thoughts was gathered on my poor lone hunted self. The little lady on the left was reserved-looking, long-faced a trifle, almost colourless, her lips too thin, too cosey shut. Her sister was pleasanter, more easily read; she was the blossom that had caught the sunshine, the relics of long-faded roses were still in her cheeks, and her eye was lively. The paler lady had no trouble at all in keeping her gaze on the bleak fields running by, but after a hundred little twitchings, ahems, stirrings, the plump little lady suddenly swept her eyes full upon me, at the same time delicately drawing the tip of a very slight little flimsy handkerchief to and fro several times along her still ruddy little lips. She found me, of course, lost in a brown study.

They were both a little birdlike of aspect, they always are! —but this old lady now surveying me, with some surprise, I warrant, was a song bird that would impulsively burst (in her youth, of course) into trills and runs and cadenzas, if only an unexpected gush of sunbeams fell on her as she walked in the fields, while her sister, I thought to myself, could not do with less than a branch of waxen candles and a little crowd of well-mannered ladies and gentlemen about her before her careful notes would fall—perhaps with unexpected passion—from her rather firm lips. Poor old chits— they had rubbed through the long years, never agreeing in anything, never exactly of the same mind, pertly impossible, often frankly offensive to each other—they could not guess how much one thing they were to me.

I saw now that while I had been riding pell-mell through the bright morning, seemingly reckless, the sense of danger, the need for alertness had been more and more becoming the whole of me, knotting me up, as it were. I remembered how when I had, unapprehended, flung myself into the train and found it begin to move off, I remembered the "Thank God" that had fallen from my lips, and, now so quietly to recall it, I felt myself opening out from that knot of care, opening out, spreading myself as a plant after the night is over, ready to drink in whatever sun and winds there may be abroad. And there before my eyes were this pair of sister-birds—

either a puzzle if the other were not by. They were a gift from a quiet old world that had not been mine for a very long time. The pair of them there between me and the dull wintry landscape on which the colourless dusk was falling, lifting, falling, lifting—they were like an old-fashioned melody—not insistent, not emotional, not headlong, just a gentle singing, a soft rhythm, with a pensive undersong, with little to say except that all roughness and noise and haste and danger were better forgotten for ever and ever. Only once did they speak. The brighter little lady said:—

" 'Tis a very dull evening, very dull."

And the other gravely nodded her head. But I found myself smiling, and saying "Dull!—No! no!—'Tis a sweet old evening—I am winging to my *gradh geal*, to my bright love, though you do not suspect it, nor do you suspect how much more keenly, ardently, passionately I will drink her into me for your sitting here beside me in your withered maidenhood."

At the next station in a flutter of colour and laughter and swift, long-gloved, white-gloved hands there broke in upon our quietness two young girls—of whom one was called Mamie and the other Lil—as we were all presently to know. They were richly befurred and wrapped, hidden away almost; for all that, however, one caught sight of dainty flesh, dainty ribbons, creamy whiteness, linen-whiteness, soft pinks, little bits of flashing jewellery, too, and very bright, frankly-youthful eyes. But it was rather their swift glances, their unhidden excitement, their meaningless yet significant words and phrases that best told what fun they were after. It is a country of big, square-built houses, and quite certainly one of them would be blazing with lights and throbbing with dancing couples this night behind its screen of branchy, silent trees.

Mamie, the younger, could not keep still; and when her fresh, musical voice leaped out upon us every cell of her healthy, warm, exhilarated being was living in it.

"Oh!—I do hope Dickie will not fail us!—He won't? he won't?" She was staring up in the face of her sister, who sat opposite her.

"You can't trust him," a voice far quieter, paler, answered, the lips alone moving.

There was a silence, the bright eyes withdrawn from her sister's face were busy with some vision of their own.

"I know what he'll say . . . Oh!" There was a silvery laugh, running off into a boyish chuckle.

"Yes." The laugh was not answered, only the words.

"He'll say, 'Do you remember that night at Bransby's?'"

A soft look of comprehension lit up the quieter eyes of the taller girl. "Yes," she answered again.

"And I'll say . . . Oh! oh!" She was choking with laughter, lowering her face into all her pink, linen and creamy mantlings.

"You'd never guess what I'll say?"

"Be quiet, Mamie."

"I'll say: 'What night at Bransby's?' 'I was never at——'"
She could not finish for laughing.

"'Sh. Be quiet. You mustn't. . . . He'd . . .'"

"And the stupid! he'll lift up his eyebrows, you know. He'll say, 'Haw!' three times. 'Haw! Haw! Haw!'" She spoke them with an effort at self-mastery, very quietly in Dickie's voice, except the last, which fell into her own.

How my two old birds—oh, they had aged immensely!—were watching, were listening!

"He's stupider than Will, but he's nicer, he's much nicer. I like him much better, I love him!"

Lily's quiet eyes glanced with some touch of shame in them towards the old ladies—had they heard? And Mamie's reckless glance followed, and, at what she saw, Dickie suddenly seemed to fall quite out of her mind. She was frankly examining now one, now the other of the two faded sisters, her thoughts passing quite legibly across her face. Who are they? Where are they going? What makes her do that? The other is doing it now. Are they cold? Were they there when we come in? Poor old things, you're very queer-looking, though I don't know what's the matter with you . . . Then quite suddenly she turned from them, and caught up Will and Dickie again. "Yes, for he's not conceited, and Will is, he's as conceited as a poll-parrot. I know; because the night——"

But Lily's dainty shoe stretched out in a little petulant kick, and the other shrugged her shoulders, and swept us all again with a glance full of inquiry: You're not listening? It doesn't matter whether you are or not—not a bit. . . . Then she suddenly leaped from her place and flattened her nose on the window-pane.

We were entering a little sideway station: the train was screaming. She swooped again upon us:—

"Here we are, old Lil! Hurry, girl, hurry!"

She was again at the window, and again she turned to us, this time with a great change in her voice: it was low, hushed with surprise.

"Lil, 'tis . . . John!"

The gentler girl, on hearing the word, stood suddenly upright, and the voice in which she spoke was fuller, richer, than her sister's had been; how could a voice so change!

" 'Tisn't? Mamie! Mamie!"

Mamie was again looking at her.

"I'm sure. 'Tis, 'tis, Lil."

"Oh! Mamie——" Then there was a whispering, and both began, nervously, quickly, to gather their wraps and little parcels together.

I opened the door for them. The younger girl leaped down and shook hands with a young man. He swung from her and folded the quieter girl in his arms, passionately and without a word.

I saw that. I stood upright myself, I do not know what gesture I made, nor if I said any words, in Irish or English. I
found myself standing, swaying, for the train was again
travelling, my hat in one hand, my other hand straying somehow over my head, my forehead. And I knew I was frighten-
ing the old ladies.

"Excuse me," I said, huskily. "I got a dizziness, a dizziness."

"If you sit down?"

"Yes." I sat down. I was trembling.

A few moments afterwards I was telling myself that it was
time I had put my work from me, when the sight of two lovers, strangers to me, embracing on a country platform, had
so played upon me.

It was six months since I had last seen Eileen MacCarthy;
six months full of tragedies, of shootings, of imprisonments
since last I had held her in my arms.

I would hold her in my arms this night! A great ecstasy
seized me. I felt the train whirling me along—whirling a
thing not entirely conscious. It was also whirling along two
old maiden ladies. That I knew. But they were far away from
me. . . . The rapture passed. They were still here before me.
I should love to help them—if only one could!

And then I began to think that the two stages of this journey had been like two movements in a sonata—the first a pensive, quiet movement; the second, a movement far brighter,
yet still reminiscent somehow of the first, except for that suddenly swift and passionate close. And as I thought of this I
found myself staring at the old ladies, as one might stare at
two children who had not yet put their teeth in that fruit we
call life—and my lips were moving in silent speech. "But
there'll be a third movement—Oh, yes! There'll be a third
movement, brighter, swifter, deeper,—it has begun, it has
begun. . . ."

And I was already glowing with the thought of it, something was surging within me; this night I would make certain that Eileen MacCarthy would be my wife for ever. These times, these times of terror and partings and jailings and sudden deaths were not times for delaying in, and. . . .

Anyway I am glad to remember I had the grace to bid the old ladies good-bye as I leaped from the train.

I rushed for my bicycle. The station, I noted gleefully, was empty of all policemen. I was soon on the dark road riding along. I saw the lighted-up train curve away in the distance, its bright plumes of cloud breaking into fragments; I heard its rhythm begin to merge into the night.

The clouds were gone. The sky was spangled all over with wide-eyed stars: how beautiful among them were the frost-still branchy treetops! I breathed deeply, deeply. I was drinking a cup full of joy in a night of serene and stately beauty.

My two old ladies were still journeying on: now they were chattering, I hoped; how colourless their version of this short journey would be—poor souls, whose eyes had never opened! Mamie and Lily were now whirling and laughing in a swift dance in that lighted-up old square house within its park of solemn trees. I did not envy them. There was room for all. Truly night is a deep womb . . . "deeper than day-light thought," as the German poet puts it. Soon . . .

"Halt! Who goes there? Halt! Get down . . . we'll fire!" The voice was roaring, I felt my knees weaken, grow cold. "Right. We're right."

A whistle was blown. I heard rifles grounded. I was caught. The policemen at the first railway station were not half so unobservant as I had thought.

That night I spent in a lonely cell in Cork jail, pacing it, pacing it, disentangling a hundred thoughts, a hundred anxieties. Gradually the heat went from my brain, and I sat down on the edge of my bed. I tried to reckon what time was. It was about two o'clock. The silence was appalling. Far away, I heard the scream of a distant train.

The Return

....

I

WHERE Ankle Lane joins Blarney Street there are four high houses, dark-looking and very old, of that sort lane-dwellers call "fabrics" or "castles." The number of inhabitants varies from day to day: tricky-men in for the races will stay two nights, cattle-drovers only one; in periods of idleness a group of coal-porters sometimes attains to a certain solidarity—the same figures go in and out the doors day after day—but, just as happens in a factory, change sets in with prosperity; new faces come and go; and the next period of idleness sees a new colony, the same in its general characteristics, though made up of quite different individuals, repeat the fortunes of the last.

The largest, the darkest of these four houses was kept by a widow named Tynan; Bonnety Tynan she was called, from a wisp of a bonnet that clung to her scanty hairs; the other lodging-house keepers wore shawls. Her face was crabbed, shut like a fist against craft, reduced to its smallest and toughest by dint of years of hard-dealing. And her bonnet was equally shorn of its beams; this, too, was now not much bigger than a fist, but the legend still held that it was the lodging-house keeper's money-box. Sometimes she would have as many as thirty men under her roof, most of them idle, so her hardness, her aloofness were needed. How else could she have managed them? The Law?—it was too complicated; and besides, she kept too irregular a house to care to

153

invoke it. She had laws and ejectment-processes of her own. Sometimes she conceived suspicion of a lodger; she waited till his back was turned; then she would slap a few buckets of water over his bed; he returned to find it sodden; and she went on with her washing while he stamped and cursed.

In the beginning of winter one evening towards six o'clock, as she shuffled in along the dark hall, she was surprised to see a glare of firelight breaking out towards her from the kitchen; she had been out of the house for some hours and hoped for nothing better than a spark in the bottom of the grate.

Opening the squeaking door she was still more surprised: a great figure, a darkness, sat on a stool before the fire; she noticed the curving width of his back; the huge head bent forward—he was asleep. She went silently up to him, bending to see his face: it was tanned; she glanced at his hands: they were dark with tar, knobby, and had blue rings and flags tattooed on them; but it was the hard, exaggerated-looking creases in his serge clothes that spoke his trade most clearly—these clothes had been folded tightly for weeks, perhaps for months, in the bottom of a seaman's chest. She shook him: "Come on now—wake up, who are 'oo? who are 'oo?"

He growled; then his voice softened; he rose and stretched himself, very much at his ease; a light came into his sea-bleared eyes; he examined the old woman's face with interest, with amusement apparently. "You're not changed a ha'-p'orth," he said, "not a ha'p'orth."

She stared up; he was handsome in such a place.

"Sit down," she said, "I can't call to mind what your name is—'tis after escaping me memory."

With a seaman's licence he put his great arm about her, drew her towards the glowing fire, and said again:

"You're not changed a ha'p'orth."

"I don't know you," she snapped out, breaking away.

"If you don't there's not a soul in Cork to say who I am—I'm Jim Daunt that was."

A memory or two, quite unimportant, stirred in her brain:

"So you are, so you are; you're welcome; how long will you be staying?"

"Till half-past eleven, anyway," he said.

"Where's the boat—Queenstown?"

"No—the Jetties," he answered, "and I must be aboard for midnight."

II

She treated him well; she gave him a couple of eggs and many rounds of bread; yet for a seaman he made but a scanty meal.

"You're not doing well?" she said.

"If I only had it yesterday," he said, "you'd see the death I'd give it."

She moved about in the silent way of a woman who is accustomed to keep people at a distance. It was he who spoke:

"Isn't this a quare thing," he said, "I was never a bit lonesome wherever I was on sea or land—thousands of miles away—never a bit lonesome till this evening sitting there on that there stool."

She believed him; for she knew these sailormen well; and how any shelter that has the look, or even the name of home, stirs them.

"You were a great long time out," he continued, half complaining.

"How did I know you'd be here?"

"When did you leave the house?"

"Near four, I expect."

"Well, now, look at that," he said. "You mustn't have been well round the corner when I came in; and here I stopped, for I couldn't go away again—couldn't go away. Was I asleep when you came in?"

A lodger they called Brother entered; Mrs. Tynan made the two men known to each other. The sailorman wanted drink to be sent for; Bonnety, however, wouldn't have it: there was plenty of time, and, besides, drink was no food for a man after a day's work. Brother seconded her; Saturday Night would be coming in soon, and he was the best of company; 'twas company a man wanted after being shut up for months in a wind-bag, "Wasn't it, matey?" he said, taking the seaman's hand. A radiance had come into Brother's face: unexpected joy is straight from the hands of the gods: exhausted, heavy in all his limbs from climbing with a laden hod forty-foot ladders from early morning—terrible work—he had hoped for nothing beyond a single drink in Miss Nora's, and lo! the pleasures of a revel were emerging in his imagination.

"Have you enough of it?" he said.

"Of what?"

"The say?"

"God knows an' I have," said the sailor, with unexpected earnestness, "but isn't it a quare thing to say that I was never a bit lonesome till this evening sitting there on that there stool?"

"How so?" said Brother.

And then with lingering detail the sailor told how he had kept watch while Mrs. Tynan was down in Miss Nora's.

III

Saturday Night came in after a few moments; in every feature, in every limb he had become misshapen by dint of combat; his most restful attitude challenged; yet in Brother's words he was the best of company: spirit is spirit.

Brother, introducing the men, mentioned the sailor's former connection with the house: "There's no house like the old house," he said, and Saturday Night, gripping the sailor's hand, told him that though he had never met him before, he felt they were old friends already: "There's something draws me to you," he said, and the sailor answered: "A fellow don't hear words like them from foreigners."

And three minutes afterwards he told Saturday Night that he had never known what it was to be down-hearted till that evening, sitting on that there stool before the fire. And, indicating Brother, "Himself will tell you," he answered Saturday Night's look of inquiry.

Again he wanted to send out for drink; but again the landlady blanked the proposal: "What hurry was there? wasn't the night long enough? couldn't they wait for Johnny Swaine at least?"

Instead of Johnny Swaine came Katty Sullivan, saying as her first word:

"Isn't Johnny here?"

"Not yet," and they bade her sit down.

"By James, I might as well," she said: the form of swear she had invented herself, and its use seemed to lift her above the common throng; yet she needed no such aid; by nature she was above her surroundings. Strong and happy, with full, firm flesh, her face coloured like ripe corn, her eyes blue and bright as the skies that go with it, she was large-hearted, and merry and frank because of her fearlessness, of her consciousness of power.

"Here's a lonely sailorman wouldn't object to a bit of company," said Saturday Night, and " 'tis a thing no wan objects to," she answered, in a tone that had as much daring as pity in it. Her words seemed to take the sailorman off his guard; the impudence in his face withered before her eyes. She had laid her spell on him; but everyone saw that some weakness of spirit denied his rising to it: he looked like a sick sportsman who, on a morning of sunshine, suddenly discovers that he is unable to lift his body from the bed. The moment's unrest was swallowed in a whirl of words, for Katty Sullivan was one they all liked to talk with. She was one of those who, though they might give a man a "wipe" across the mouth, never get on their dignity, an attitude that takes all heart out of a night's merriment. Soon Johnny Swaine came seeking Katty, even as she had been seeking him; and the sailor saw at once that he was her accepted lover, and with the knowledge a touch of daring came back into his look; his eyes, in spite of himself, as it were, would now find themselves resting on Johnny's face. Brother was sent for drink; he returned with two friends; " 'twould go to me heart to refuse them," he explained to the sailor.

The sailor drank nothing but raw whiskey, and it soon appeared that his loneliness had gone from him; so, too, had his hold on himself. He became aggressive; when Brother was telling his champion tale of a sailor who, having deserted, signed on again in the self-same ship under stress of drink, the sailor stopped him half-way, and in his mouth the story from being a mere fill-gap became wild and thrilling. And almost without a pause he went on to tell the story of a parson's daughter of Adelaide, the girl who hid herself in a ship's hold for the sake of a young captain—how she might now be met with in the cities of the South American seaboard, in Buenos Ayres or Rio—the sailors speak of her as the Australian Rose. He had seen her himself. His voice became higher and louder; he seemed to be talking against time, and his eyes shifted continually from face to face. He twitted Brother on his powers of drinking; he joked Saturday Night on his wounds; yet somehow his merriment was not contagious; and they all sniffed trouble when he began to raise bad blood between the lovers, for they could see that Katty's eyes were rife for mischief.

Johnny, she said, would have gone sailoring himself only for the wetness of the sea and his love for his mother; anyway, he wouldn't like to be pickled as well as drownded and, by James! she wouldn't care to see him pickled herself; "he'd be a terrible sight!" Then the sailor, with great concern, asked her what would she do if Johnny went off with another girl? She laughed, bent with laughter at the idea, and the whole room laughed uneasily with her. And so Johnny Swaine, made scapegoat for the company, sat by the girl's side, looking with glum eyes at his unfinished drink. But at the end of a bout of merriment the sailor stretched his hand to him saying that a joke was a joke; Johnny would not even look at the proffered hand. "Anyway, fetch us the measure," the sailor continued with some diplomacy; and Swaine, thinking of peace with honour, rose from his place and made for the gallon. Without a sound the sailor sprang into the vacant space at the girl's side, and Johnny, turning, found him there. A roar of laughter addled him, maddened him. He flung the gallon about the floor, squared out, and his voice rose above the jubilee: "Stand up, if you're a man."

"Miss Sullivan," the sailor's voice was heard saying in the sudden, expectant silence, "isn't it lovely weather?"

"Stand up, I say."

"A beautiful night?"

"Will you stand up?"

And the girl's eyes danced to see such spirit in her lover.

"You won't, won't you?" and Johnny's open hand met the sailor's cheek with a ringing blow. In a flash the two men were dancing at each other, the sailor all activity, his voice jerking out the best known of all the chanties:

> Ranzo was no sailor;
> Ranzo, boys, Ranzo.

And every time he came to "Ranzo" in the refrain—the word on which the rope is dragged as they hoist sail—he struck or rather touched Johnny's face or side or ears: he played with the landsman, dancing round him, tipping him wherever he wished.

> Ranzo was no sailor;
> Ranzo, boys, Ranzo.

> The mate he was a good man;
> Ranzo, boys, Ranzo!

The company seeing that he did not mean to punish his man let their mirth loose; they began to cry out: "Go it, Johnny, go it, old man." But after some time the sailor became over-confident, became careless; Johnny, on the other hand, had recovered his self-possession. Seeing a chance, he stood statue-still for a moment; then, making a wild charge, struck full in the sailor's face. The sea-blood fired up; song and dance ceased; with swift, careful drives he drove Johnny back, back, almost into the fire-grate. The room had become silent. Both men seemed to be fighting for life. They panted; their feet scraped the floor. Katty stood up: "Sir," she said, in a breathy voice that was scarcely audible, "Sir, sir"; but neither fighters nor onlookers heard her at all.

Suddenly shuffling steps were heard coming in the hall, and "Police," whispered Brother; for policemen walk into such houses in the same manner as factory-inspectors enter factories. At the word the sailor's face went white; he turned half-round from his man towards the room door; and Johnny, who had not perhaps heard Brother's warning, battered him right and left with great will.

"Wait awhile," said the sailor, all confusion, still staring at the door.

"Come on," shouted Johnny, wondering what had happened.

All faces were on the door; some of the men were gripping others by the shoulders. It was old Ned Mulcahy, the mason, who stuck in his head. The next moment the sailor was dancing once more around Johnny.

> He gave him five and twenty;
> Ranzo, boys, Ranzo.

His terror had lifted; he resumed his antics, and soon he had Johnny hemmed into a corner, where he kept him until he had his nose pumping blood. Then the combatants were separated.

"He's a game fighter, anyway," said the sailor, releasing him; and Katty Sullivan, passing the defeated man a handkerchief, thought in her heart of hearts that she wouldn't give him for all the tanned-faced sailors on the sea.

IV

It was now high time for the sailor to be going if he was to make his ship by midnight; yet he dawdled to hear the end of a story, to turn a joke, to look at Johnny's nose. He lingered too long; for Saturday Night suddenly began to tell the tale he always reserved till he had become quite emotional in his drink. They were unloading the "Cyclamen," he said, and the first glimmer of dawn was coming on the river and, merciful God! he saw a woman floating down the tide, her golden hair spread out on top of the water. They got her into a boat—the handsomest woman he ever laid eyes on, and he tried to persuade the men to say nothing at all about the matter, only just take the corpse up to Burnt Lane on a shutter and give her a decent wake with candles, and Christian burial in the Gardens; but they wouldn't, they were afraid of the law; and the police came, and the first words the sergeant said were (and Saturday Night wept to repeat them): "What do you know about this *person?*" "What do you know about this *person?*" Saturday Night spoke the words again, turning towards the sailor; and "Was that what he said?" the sailor gasped out, but his voice was so strange that the whole room on the instant forgot the story; the sailor's jaw had become locked, his neck rigid, his head looked as if carved in hardwood, the eyes unskilfully painted—a blank stare. But he lifted himself up, and "I'll be late," he said, in a voice that beseeched them not to question or hinder him; he had broken down; he could not explain himself—at least, this is what they would think.

"Good night," he said, putting out his hand to Katty Sullivan in a sudden, jerky way, his eyes meanwhile turned away from all the faces. She took no notice; she let on to be speaking to Johnny, who was now once more at her side. Without another word the sailor vanished from their midst.

After a pause the old woman spoke in her hardest voice: "Did any of ye see that fellow coming in here?"

No one spoke; in the silence Brother cracked a match on the bowl of his pipe.

"He said he came in here to-day after I wint out."

"And sure he might."

"I'd like to know," the old woman rejoined, and she lit two candles—a signal for them to retire.

"He said he was asleep," she added, "he was no more asleep than I was."

"Holy Mother!" said Katty Sullivan, as she rose to go, "I'm sorry I iver laid eyes on him."

V

Now, I think that the sailor, as he stumbled down the deserted hillside streets towards the river, shook himself and stood still a moment here, stood still a moment elsewhere, saying at every pause: " 'Twill be all right—what a fool I am!"

Anyway, he got to his ship; made to walk up the plank with his head in the air, and—who knows how the end came?

But the next day they brought up two dead bodies from between his ship and the quay-wall; one of them, the second mate it was, had a knife-wound in the right lung and another in the back below the lung; the second body, bearing no signs of struggle on it, was our sailorman, Jim Daunt; and it was proved by the stopping of their watches and otherwise that one body had been a couple of hours longer in the water than the other. Saturday Night says that as he went up the plank maybe he heard a voice saying "What do you know about this *person*?" but Brother says that 'tis how he threw himself in, for he saw that the whole race of men were turning against him—look at how Katty Sullivan, with no reason at all, *couldn't* shake hands with him. Johnny Swaine says they all came well out of it, as if a murderer has evil spirits at his beck and call.

But what brought the sailorman up to Bonnety Tynan's at all? Was he trying to prove an alibi? Or was it that the word Home was ringing in his brain?

Vanity

....

I

FROM that great mountain-wall which divides Cork from Kerry great spurs of broken and terraced rock run out on the Cork side like vast buttresses; and in the flanks of these great buttresses are round-ended glens, or cooms, as they are called in Irish. Those on the northern flanks of such spurs are gloomy beyond belief.

The dwellers in these cold valleys are of such an austere, puritanic type that the exception among them who is given to the vanities of the world shows out with indescribable, if unholy lustre. In Lyrenascaul old Diarmuid MacCoitir was such a man; it may be more correct to say, had been such a man, for he was now of great age and confined to his bed. In the little dark back-room,—it was dark because a sheer slab of rock, grey, lichened, and damp, rose up behind the house, —he passed the long hours of day and night. Between the darkness of the room itself and the darkness that was coming over his eyes, there was not much difference for him now between day and night, except that in the day he could still hear the little stir of life—very little indeed it was—that went on around the miserable bit of a farm, which he had made over to his son. In the few other houses that clung against the sides of Lyrenascaul there were here and there other bed-ridden ancients; these you beheld with their beads in their hands, night as well as day, and a certain pallor, a quiet

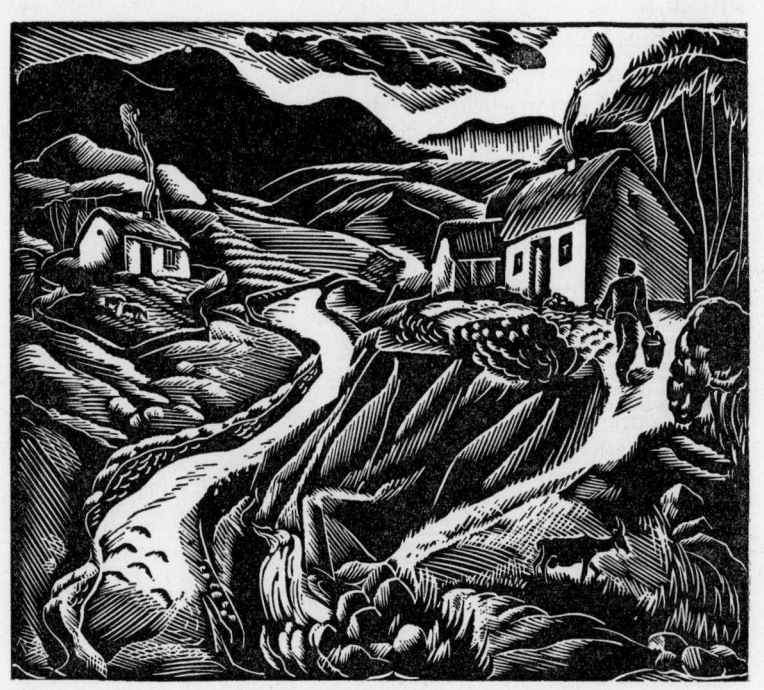

peacefulness that lay always on their features, told you they had long since put this world aside and were now calmly awaiting the call to the next world.

Diarmuid had never been of the same mind as these; and instead of that great calmness of theirs, it would be a thick sort of smile would come slowly crawling over his features, sometimes holding them for quite long spells.

He lived there with his wife, who was almost as old as himself and as unworldly as he was worldly; and the only other person in the house was their only remaining son, the still unmarried Michael, now an old man himself, one too who had inherited much of the worldliness and hardness of the ancient who day after day lay bed-ridden in the little dark back-room.

Into that out-of-the-world coom—it was miles from any main road—it was seldom a stray newspaper from Cork or Dublin made its way. You might even to-day live there a long six months and not see one; and I am told that many people easily remember the time when no papers at all entered, with their strange tales of the outside world. Old Diarmuid could not read (indeed his son could hardly do as much) but even if he could what interest would he have found in the news of a world he had never been in, more especially when that news would consist of a series of unrelated facts, with, for him, no yesterday, no to-morrow? News of fairs and markets he might have fathomed, if there were any such. There usually was not. In every paper, however, that chanced to find its way into that forgotten world, there would be a series of paragraphs that always came home to him and gripped his thoughts—these were the death notices. For many years these notices were such a novelty that he learned each of them by heart from some other person's reading, and would recite the latest to his gossips, and compare it with ones he had earlier learned, and go on to speak of the difference between one which mentioned that a Re-

quiem Mass had been sung and one which was content with
the modest: R.I.P.

At that stage he was, when, without warning, he was one
day struck with a stroke of paralysis. He took to his bed. One
evening he sat up, thinking of what had befallen him. He
called to his son:

"Hi!" he said, "Michael, Michael!"

Michael had been chopping furze to give as food to their
poor sorry nag; he came in, chopper in hand:

"Well?"

"Tell me this, Michael, if twas dead you found me this
day, or any other day, would you put a little biteen of a notice in the paper—just a little biteen of a wan with R.I.P.
at the end of it?"

Michael looked at him and noticed how strong and sturdy
he was. He smiled, not sweetly or lovingly. He threw an eye
around the dark, almost empty little house, he took a step
to the open door and glanced with scorn at the scraggy patch
of land that was their farm; he came back and said:

"Isn't it well you deserve it from me?"

"Don't be hard, Michael, boy, there's a good time coming; you won't have to face what I had to face, the struggling
with landlords, and the law—the law, that would leave a
rich man poor and a poor man broken. Give me your word,
Michael, boy, when it pleases God to call me you'll put a
little biteen of a notice in the paper so that—"

"I won't then give you me word. An old man like you, 'tis
something else should be troubling you besides having your
name stuck in the paper and you cold on the bed—" And
then, just as he was about to begin his furze-chopping again,
he called out:

"Was there ever anyone from Lyrenascaul in the paper
and he dead?"

"That's why!" said the old man, sitting up suddenly, while
quite a glow came back into his heavy face.

Not long after there did really happen to be a death-notice from Lyrenascaul in the paper. It was American gold put it there. Old John Kevane had died. The news had been leisurely enough sent to his son in America. A few days after its arrival there the notice appeared in the Cork and Dublin papers—cabled from America! Whereupon old Diarmuid MacCoitir renewed his importunity, not, however, with more success, "There's a great fear of you dying, a great fear indeed!" his son would answer, and pass the thing off as a joke.

II

It was long after midnight when the old man heard his son's horse-and-cart jolting up the rock-strewn bohereen. In that dead hour he could hear it even when a great way off. He had not expected Michael earlier, he had been at Inchigeela fair. Some little brightness came into the dull face to hear the sound of the wheels. That fair day used to be a bright feature in his own life in the days now gone for ever; he thought it meant the same for his son, as in some measure it did; and with each recurrence of the event some little trace of his old alertness would struggle up in the old man's face, and that unlovely smile was sure to follow. After long waiting he heard the son putting up his horse. He entered and his face was a great broad smile.

" 'Tis a queer thing I'm after hearing this day," he said to his father.

"What was it?" and the old man scanned his son's face, rather pleased, perhaps, as well as a little jealous, to find in it the excitement and jollity of strong drink.

"What was it?" he said.

"Well, then, 'tis this: I'm after learning, and from good authority, that if yourself and herself died together on the wan day on me I'd get a notice in the paper for the same money as if it was only one of ye was in it!" And he sat on a stool, with one gaiter dangling in his hand, and he laughed stupidly, and with such loudness as seemed sacrilegious in that solemn mountain glen, in that great darkness and silence.

"Wouldn't ye do it, and I promise ye, ye'd get it—the notice!"

"Do what?"

"Die, the pair of ye, on the wan day!"

The old man growled at him and turned away. The son went off in a great fit of laughter. Likely enough his horse had often heard him laugh that night as he came the long twenty-seven miles of bogland and mountain. And the great joke held him for several weeks!

Although he had answered not a word, this new idea took possession of the old man's mind. But whereas formerly in those odd moments when in imagination he would behold his neighbours passing the paper which contained his own death-notice from hand to hand, he always felt nothing but joy and pride, now there was in the dream some shadowy fear he could not fathom, could not put aside. There was certainly no feeling of pride left in him. In fact he soon came to trying to avoid the vision; it had now, however, become part of himself, so keenly had he desired it, so frequently had he indulged it. He could not avoid it. At any moment of great stillness it would suddenly stand before him—a group of his neighbours—old Padraig Lynch, old Tadhg Cremin, old Steve Casey, with his one eye, old Morty Shea, with his high, white forehead and glasses—there they were, all gathered together around the Master while he read out to them "At their son's residence in Lyrenascaul, at an advanced age, Jeremiah and Mary Cotter. . . ." Ah! that was it: there were now always the two names coupled together in the death-notice he beheld his neighbours reading. Yet in spite of his new-sprung hatred he couldn't banish the vision, couldn't prevent its re-appearance at the most unexpected hours.

If he woke up in the still night what else was there for him to think about? In fact it seemed as if he had been waked up for the one purpose of seeing the vision, as if indeed the vision had been waiting for him to awaken. In great and terrifying clearness there was Morty Shea, that calm, saintly-looking man with the white forehead and the glasses, there was Steve Casey, with the one eye, a black slit where the other should be, listening, intently listening; there, too, was——. All joy had passed away out of old Diarmuid's mind.

When his wife, who was now almost ninety, he himself was ninety-three, brought in a ponny of milk to him he would strain whatever sight he had left to look slyly up in her face; he would also pass his hand over hers—he was glad if it felt distinctly hotter or distinctly colder; he was depressed if it seemed the same as his own. He would make sly inquiries of his son as to how she was in health.

It was another fair day, a mellow harvest-golden day in September; the son was again from home. He would not be home till late. Towards evening the old woman brought in some milk and home-made bread to the bed-ridden man. They had nothing to say to one another. They were too old. She waited till he had finished, she then carried out the vessels again. He settled himself for a comfortable sleep; he would then wake up refreshed and be ready to receive the news of the fair; it had become a point of honour with him to be awake on such occasions. He had not been long asleep when he awoke with a curious tingling sensation, and there was that terrible vision once again, the same faces, the same attitudes. And he was disturbed. He should not have awakened so soon.

"Maire!" he called out in his wheezy voice.

He got no answer.

"Maire! Maire! I'm queer."

There was no sound, except the water running down that slab of rock behind the house.

"Maire! Maire!"

Even while he called, it was of his own fear he was thinking. And then, horribly real—the people in the vision began to move, a hand was lifted, an eye turned—

. . . .

"Don't forget the R.I.P., Master," said their son. "If that wasn't in it he wouldn't be satisfied, even how long we made it."

"I have R.I.P. in it."

"Read it now."

"At their son's residence, Lyrenascaul, Jeremiah and Mary ——"

Storm-Struck

....

I

O N AN August afternoon the fishing village of Cuandor
on the west Cork coast is like a dream-village; it is
so still. Its rocky street is then a strip of sunshine, a
strip of shadow; and not a soul crosses from the one to the
other: the men are far on the sea, they have sailed in their
nobbies and ketches for the Manx fishing-grounds; and the
women are at work in their gardens, bent over the violets
they grow in ridges, like potatoes, for the London markets.

On such a day John Donovan arrived home from Butte
City, Montana. It looked as if he had stolen home. Even
so, the news was not long spreading from hedge to hedge—
an empty story.

Nightfall brought no relief. Instead of his coming into
Lavelle's public-house, there came Jack Kiniry from Ringo-
greine. On his way he had passed the Donovans' house, and
his tale was that the place was dark and silent. And as he
said so, his questioners saw it in vision—a windy, stony place,
just where the good land ended and the cliffs began. Because it was so poor, the boy, John Donovan, had sailed six
years before for America.

The following day was Sunday. The church bell had tolled
for Mass; yet still, as was customary, the dark-cloaked women
and the sun-tanned men from the hills lingered in groups.
They whispered in low voices that the boy of the Donovans'

had come home—a blinded man. But when, at the end of
the rocky street, the group they had waited for appeared, the
blind man and his aged father, the peasants moved silently
into the church, where already the priest was praying on the
altar.

As the old man, bent almost double from years and the
slavery of his toil, led his son over the uneven ground, he
looked up from under his brows, to right, to left, and spoke no
word. He looked like one who had done something wrong.
But his son was more than erect, his head flung nervously up
in that sorry posture common to blind men and dreamers, his
blank eyes sweeping equally landscape and sky and sea.

This had Butte City, Montana, done for him. A flash of
light in the gloom of a copper mine, a rumble, a tremor; then,
silence. Afterwards, amid a whispering of nun-like voices,
the gradual return of consciousness in a bed of snow-white
sheets, snow-white to judge by the feel of them. "I want to
go home," he whined, like a boy who fails half-way in an ad-
venture. Then recalling the explosion, he fainted again, and,
as he did so, he heard someone whisper that his sight was
gone.

The first night at home he scarcely spoke a word. His father and mother in their lonely house had lived more or less
always in silence; and he, since his loss, had become acquainted with it. Perhaps, this first night, he was listening to
the loud ticking of the weight-clock or to the crying seagulls.
But after a long pause he blurted out: "Where's Kitty Regan
now?"

The old man and woman looked at each other, neither
quite ready to answer; they knew what Kitty Regan had
meant to him before his departure to America; they knew
why there he had chosen the slavery of the copper-mines and
had hoarded his earnings. The father thought it better to
speak carelessly, as if it now was all an old story:

"Oh, she married into Kilvonane parish."

"I thought so," said the blind man.

And in spite of his effort at control a quiver crossed his face, such as might happen in a dream. It went through his mother like a sword. She rose, putting an arm around his shoulder, laying her hand on his:

"Don't mind, boy," she said: "maybe 'tis she wasn't worthy of you—and look at the man she got; God help us, 'tis a hard life she has." And the mother pressed the son to her breast.

He sprang to his feet.

"What's this? Bless me! We're not going to have scenes, sure we're not."

And forgetting himself, he flung forward from her hands and fell on the chair she had risen from. Steadying himself, he cursed several times in a voice that was hard and strange to them; it was his Butte City voice.

At first he took to sitting outside the door in the sunshine, and by dint of short and bitter answers soon rid himself of the gossips of the place. It seemed he could satisfy himself for ever with listening to the seagulls and rooks. However, after some weeks, he made friends with a boy named Conny Maher, and the two of them would go for long rambles on the cliff-tops. One day they got as far as Fylenashouk, the most windy, the highest of all the cliffs; and ever afterwards this was his favourite resting-place. It stands sheer above the sea: eastwards there is the long promontory running out to the Galley Head, in summer time a strip of gold terminating in a white point; westwards the coast is fringed with groups of rocky islets, pearly in the sun. Perhaps he remembered west and east in the touch of the wind.

One day in the late autumn, sitting there alone, he felt the sun darken; then a large rain-drop stabbed the back of his hand. In a second the whole shower was pelting on him. He bent his head waiting for it to pass; but the whole face of the day had changed—afar off he heard the dull rolling of thunder. He began to fidget. Carefully he stood up, crouching his

back to the rain. He must not move, he might walk over the cliff; besides, Conny would soon come seeking him. But, as if it had leaped through a great distance of space, the thunder suddenly crashed about him. "My God!" he said, listening to its rolling off. "Conny, Conny," he then cried out, and anger and anxiety struggled in his throat. Again and again he started, feeling that lightnings were playing about him. And "Conny, Conny," he screamed between the thunderclaps.

Unexpectedly a hand, wet with rain, caught his, and a coarse voice, yet a woman's voice, said "Come." Hastily they made forward over the rough ground, so hastily indeed that soon his breath went from him, and in spite of the rain he grew hot and sweaty. "Stop a moment," he gasped; "I'm bate out, 'tis long since I went so fast." He made to smile, but it flickered out at once, for he thought that he might be staring at a rock or tree. His hand had been dropped, and the stranger's silence stung him. "Do you see a little boy anywhere? Dan Maher's little boy, Conny Maher?"

"No," was the sullen answer.

"We'll go on," he said, bitterly; his blindness had never so come home to him. The stranger again gripped his hand firmly, almost fiercely, and in the same headlong haste they made on through the pouring rain. "Oh, oh," he said, whenever the thunder burst; but his helpmate kept her silence. And so he stumbled on, until his limbs were staggering and his heart thumping.

"If there's e'er a shelter anywhere, I could wait; Conny will be coming——"

"Where's the shelter?"

Drooping, he stood fetching short breaths: "You'll be all wet," he said.

"Where's the harrum in it?"

"I'm all right now," he said, and stretched out his useless hand once more.

When he found himself being dragged through some bushes he knew where he was.

"The road?" he said.

"Yes," came a gasping reply.

More swiftly now they stumbled down the hill. He was gaining hope, reckoning that his house could not be far off, when his hand was suddenly flung down, seized, and dropped again, and "Oh!" the voice cried, as if in terror, "there's someone coming," and the woman rushed from him. "Kitty, Kitty Regan, for God's sake——" he cried, all in a breath, his voice wild and high with surprise and despair, his hand glauming at nothing. Only with her last word had her own voice broken from her, letting him know whose hand had led him. Too late; there he stood, his empty hand stretched out, the rain drenching it. His father came panting up to him. "In the name of God, Shawn," he said, "how did 'oo come so far?"

"Whisht," said the blind man, struggling with his thought.

" 'Tis a miracle from God, 'tis so," said the old man, and "Whisht, I'm telling ye," was again his son's savage reply.

II

That night John Donovan sat like a dazed man in the kitchen; and outside the rain poured and winds went by howling. His presence imposed silence on the room. Twice had the old man raised his head and whispered: "God pity them that's on the sea this night," and twice his son had scowled at him. At last the old people went off, leaving him alone. He lingered for a few minutes, then taking a pine-splinter, and lighting it at the turves, he went into the little back room, lit a candle, as if he could see by its light, pulled the curtain down from the window, and sat wearily on the edge of the bed. He struggled to keep calm, but hot sweat came out all over him. Then he went cold and shivered. Worn out from stress of emotion, he would yawn in sheer exhaustion, would endeavour to calm himself, to sit still, to smile. But he could not. He rose and moved about; sat down and rose again, while the storm grabbed at his little house as if it would sweep it bodily over the cliffs; and every other moment he would stretch his ear towards the window, listening, jerking his head quickly about like a bird's. At last, muttering, he removed his boots, and was standing upright when, as if he had heard a noise outside his window, he sprang forward, quenched the light with one quick slap, flung open the window, and thrust his head, his blind head, out into the storm, whispering wild and yearning words of invitation and love. But the night was empty of companionship.

Chilled and angry, he drew back and threw himself along the bed, and grabbed at the bedclothes, rocking himself to and fro, sobbing out the one word—No! No!—over and over again, unwilling to confess defeat, unwilling to face the blank, loveless future. Yet in the end his words died away; self-pity clothed him all over with the warmth of tears; his passion ebbed, he slept.

The woman's sleep was different. Her they found next day, bedraggled, muddied, soaked, lying in a gully far back in the hills between Cuandor and Kilvonane, where her husband lived. She had been visiting her parents, had set off across the hills; the storm had overtaken her, had waylaid her. Her hands were torn, and she bled from the brow; she must have stumbled blindly on for many a mile in fright and fear. Perhaps she *had* skulked about John Donovan's house; this, anyway, was what he meant to suggest when in the crowd of gossips that gathered in Lavelle's public-house discussing the event, he began to jest about the storm-birds that seek shelter from the storm at the lighthouse-keeper's window, how they do not have the courage to enter when the window is opened to them. The gossips could not understand; they stared in wonder at his bitter lips, his stony eyes.

The Ploughing of
the Leaca

．．．

W<small>ITH</small> which shall I begin—man or place? Perhaps I had better first tell of the man; of him the incident left so withered that no sooner had I laid eyes on him than I said: Here is one whose blood at some terrible moment of his life stood still, stood still and never afterwards regained its quiet, old-time ebb-and-flow. A word or two then about the place—a sculped-out shell in the Kerry mountains, an evil-looking place, green-glaring like a sea when a storm has passed. To connect man and place together, even as they worked one with the other to bring the tragedy about, ought not then to be so difficult.

I had gone into those desolate treeless hills searching after the traces of an old-time Gaelic family that once were lords of them. But in this mountainy glen I forgot my purpose almost as soon as I entered it.

In that round-ended valley—they call such a valley a coom—there was but one farmhouse, and Considine was the name of the householder—Shawn Considine, the man whose features were white with despair; his haggard appearance reminded me of what one so often sees in war-ravaged Munster—a ruined castle-wall hanging out above the woods, a grey spectre. He made me welcome, speaking

179

slowly, as if he was not used to such amenities. At once I began to explain my quest. I soon stumbled; I felt that his thoughts were far away. I started again. A daughter of his looked at me—Nora was her name—looked at me with meaning; I could not read her look aright. Haphazardly I went through old family names and recalled old-world incidents; but with no more success. He then made to speak; I could catch only broken phrases, repeated again and again. "In the presence of God." "In the Kingdom of God." "All gone for ever." "Let them rest in peace"—(I translate from the Irish). Others, too, there were of which I could make nothing. Suddenly I went silent. His eyes had begun to change. They were not becoming fiery or angry—that would have emboldened me, I would have blown on his anger; a little passion, even an outburst of bitter temper would have troubled me but little if in its sudden revelation I came on some new fact or even a new name in the broken story of that ruined family. But no; not fiery but cold and terror-stricken were his eyes becoming. Fear was rising in them like dank water. I withdrew my gaze, and his daughter ventured on speech:

"If you speak of the cattle, noble person, or of the land, or of the new laws, my father will converse with you; but he is dark about what happened long ago." Her eyes were even more earnest than her tongue—they implored the pity of silence.

So much for the man. A word now about the place where his large but neglected farmhouse stood against a bluff of rock. To enter that evil-looking green-mountained glen was like entering the jaws of some slimy, cold-blooded animal. You felt yourself leaving the sun, you shrunk together, you hunched yourself as if to bear an ugly pressure. In the far-back part of it was what is called in the Irish language a *leaca*—a slope of land, a lift of land, a bracket of land jutting out from the side of a mountain. This leaca, which the daugh-

ter explained was called Leaca-na-Naomh—the Leaca of the
Saints—was very remarkable. It shone like a gem. It held the
sunshine as a field holds its crop of golden wheat. On three
sides it was pedestalled by the sheerest rock. On the fourth
side it curved up to join the parent mountain-flank. Huge and
high it was, yet height and size took some time to estimate,
for there were mountains all around it. When you had been
looking at it for some time you said aloud: "That leaca is
high!" When you had stared for a longer time you said: "That
leaca is immensely high—and huge!" Still the most remarkable thing about it was the way it held the sunshine. When
all the valley had gone into the gloom of twilight—and this
happened in the early afternoon—the leaca was still at mid-
day. When the valley was dark with night and the lamps had
been long alight in the farmhouse, the leaca had still the red
gleam of sunset on it. It hung above the misty valley like a
velarium—as they used to call that awning-cloth which hung
above the emperor's seat in the amphitheatre.

"What is it called, do you say?" I asked again.

"Leaca-na-Naomh," she replied.

"Saints used to live on it?"

"The Hermits," she answered, and sighed deeply.

Her trouble told me that that leaca had to do with the
fear that was burrowing like a mole in her father's heart. I
would test it. Soon afterwards the old man came by, his eyes
on the ground, his lips moving.

"That leaca," I said, "what do you call it?"

He looked up with a startled expression. He was very
white; he couldn't abide my steady gaze.

"Nora," he cried, raising his voice suddenly and angrily,
"*cas isteach iad, cas isteach iad!*" He almost roared at the
gentle girl.

"Turn in—what?" I said, roughly, "the cattle are in long
ago."

" 'Tis right they should," he answered, leaving me.

Yes, this leaca and this man had between them moulded out a tragedy, as between two hands.

Though the sun had gone still I sat staring at it. It was far off, but whatever light remained in the sky had gathered to it. I was wondering at its clear definition among all the vague and misty mountain-shapes when a voice, quivering with age, high and untuneful, addressed me:

" 'Twould be right for you to see it when there's snow on it."

"Ah!"

" 'Tis blinding!" The voice had changed so much as his inner vision strengthened that I gazed up quickly at him. He was a very old man, somewhat fairy-like in appearance, but he had the eyes of a boy! These eyes told me he was one who had lived imaginatively. Therefore I almost gripped him lest he should escape; from him would I learn of Leaca-na-Naomh. Shall I speak of him as a vassal of the house, or as a tatter of the family, or as a spall of the rough landscape? He was native to all three. His homespun was patched with patches as large and as straight-cut as those you'd see on a fisherman's sail. He was, clothes and all, the same colour as the aged lichen of the rocks; but his eyes were as fresh as dew.

Gripping him, as I have said, I searched his face, as one searches a poem for a hidden meaning.

"When did it happen, this dreadful thing?" I said.

He was taken off his guard. I could imagine, I could almost feel his mind struggling, summoning up an energy sufficient to express his idea of how as well as when the thing happened. At last he spoke deliberately.

"When the master,"—I knew he meant the householder—"was at his best, his swiftest and strongest in health, in riches, in force and spirit." He hammered every word.

"Ah!" I said; and I noticed the night had begun to thicken, fitly I thought, for my mind was already making mad leaps into the darkness of conjecture. He began to speak a more simple language:

"In those days he was without burden or ailment—unless maybe every little biteen of land between the rocks that he had not as yet brought under the plough was a burden. This, that, yonder, all those fine fields that have gone back again into heather and furze, it was he made them. There's sweat in them! But while he bent over them in the little dark days of November, dropping his sweat, he would raise up his eyes and fix them on the leaca. *That* would be worth all of them, and worth more than double all of them if it was brought under the plough."

"And why not?" I said.

"Plough the bed of the saints?"

"I had forgotten."

"You are not a Gael of the Gaels maybe?"

"I had forgotten; continue; it grows chilly."

"He had a serving-man; he was a fool; they were common in the country then; they had not been as yet herded into asylums. He was a fool; but a true Gael. That he never forgot; except once."

"Continue."

"He had also a sire horse, Griosach he called him, he was so strong, so high and princely."

"A plough horse?"

"He had never been harnessed. He was the master's pride and boast. The people gathered on the hillsides when he rode him to Mass. You looked at the master; you looked at the horse; the horse knew the hillsides were looking at him. He made music with his hoofs, he kept his eyes to himself, he was so proud."

"What of the fool?"

"Have I spoken of the fool?"

"Yes, a true Gael."

" 'Tis true, that word. He was as strong as Griosach. He

was what no one else was: he was a match for Griosach. The
master petted the horse. The horse petted the master. Both
of them knew they went well together. But Griosach the sire
horse feared Liam Ruadh the fool; and Liam Ruadh the fool
feared Griosach the sire horse. For neither had as yet found
out that he was stronger than the other. They would play
together like two strong boys, equally matched in strength
and daring. They would wrestle and throw each other. Then
they would leave off; and begin again when they had recovered their breath."

"Yes," I said, "the master, the horse Griosach, the fool
Liam—now, the Leaca, the Leaca."

"I have brought in the leaca. It will come in again, now!
The master was one day standing at a gap for a long time;
there was no one near him. Liam Ruadh came near him. 'It
is not lucky to be so silent as that,' he said. The master raised
his head and answered:

" 'The Leaca for wheat.'

"The fool nearly fell down in a sprawling heap. No one
had ever heard of anything like that.

" 'No,' he said like a child.

" 'The Leaca for wheat,' the master said again, as if there
was someone inside him speaking.

"The fool was getting hot and angry.

" 'The Leaca for prayer!' he said.

" 'The Leaca for wheat,' said the master, a third time.

"When the fool heard him he gathered himself up and
roared—a loud 'O-oh!' it went around the hills like sudden
thunder; in the little breath he had left he said: 'The Leaca
for prayer!'

"The master went away from him; who could tell what
might have happened?

"The next day the fool was washing a sheep's diseased
foot—he had the struggling animal held firm when the master slipped behind him and whispered in his ear:

" 'The Leaca for wheat.'

"Before the fool could free the animal the master was gone. He was a wild, swift man that day. He laughed. It was that self-same night he went into the shed where Liam slept and stood a moment looking at the large face of the fool working in his dreams. He watched him like that a minute. Then he flashed the lantern quite close into the fool's eyes so as to dazzle him, and he cried out harshly, 'The Leaca for wheat,' making his voice appear far off, like a trumpet-call, and before the fool could understand where he was, or whether he was asleep or awake, the light was gone and the master was gone.

"Day after day the master put the same thought into the fool's ear. And Liam was becoming sullen and dark. Then one night long after we were all in our sleep we heard a wild crash. The fool had gone to the master's room. He found the door bolted. He put his shoulder to it. The door went in about the room, and the arch above it fell in pieces around the fool's head—all in the still night.

" 'Who's there? What is it?' cried the master, starting up in his bed.

" 'Griosach for the plough!' said the fool.

"No one could think of Griosach being hitched to a plough. The master gave him no answer. He lay down in his bed and covered his face. The fool went back to his straw. Whenever the master now said 'The Leaca for wheat' the fool would answer 'Griosach for the plough.'

"The tree turns the wind aside, yet the wind at last twists the tree. Like wind and tree, master and fool played against each other, until at last they each of them had spent their force.

" 'I will take Griosach and Niamh and plough the leaca,' said the fool; it was a hard November day.

" 'As you wish,' said the master. Many a storm finishes with a little sob of wind. Their voices were now like a little wind.

"The next night a pair of smiths were brought into the coom all the way from Aunascawl. The day after that the mountains were ringing with their blows as the ploughing-gear was overhauled. Without rest or laughter or chatter the work went on, for Liam was at their shoulders, and he hardly gave them time to wipe their sweaty hair. One began to sing: ' 'Tis my grief on Monday now,' but Liam struck him one blow and stretched him. He returned to his work quiet enough after that. We saw the fool's anger rising. We made way for him; and he was going back and forth the whole day long; in the evening his mouth began to froth and his tongue to blab. We drew away from him; wondering what he was thinking of. The master himself began to grow timid; he hadn't a word in him; but he kept looking up at us from under his brow as if he feared we would turn against him. Sure we wouldn't; wasn't he our master—even what he did?

"When the smiths had mounted their horses that night to return to Aunascawl one of them stooped down to the master's ear and whispered: 'Watch him, he's in a fever.'

" 'Who?'

" 'The fool.' That was a true word.

"Some of us rode down with the smiths to the mouth of the pass, and as we did so snow began to fall silently and thickly. We were glad; we thought it might put back the dreadful business of the ploughing. When we returned towards the house we were talking. But a boy checked us.

" 'Whisht!' he said.

"We listened. We crept beneath the thatch of the stables. Within we heard the fool talking to the horses. We knew he was putting his arms around their necks. When he came out, he was quiet and happy-looking. We crouched aside to let him pass. Then we told the master.

" 'Go to your beds,' he said, coldly enough.

"We played no cards that night; we sang no songs; we thought it too long until we were in our dark beds. The last thing we thought of was the snow falling, falling, falling on Leaca-na-Naomh and on all the mountains. There was not a stir or a sigh in the house. Everyone feared to hear his own bed creak. And at last we slept.

"What awoke me? I could hear voices whispering. There was fright in them. Before I could distinguish one word from another I felt my neck creeping. I shook myself. I leaped up. I looked out. The light was blinding. The moon was shining on the slopes of new snow. There was none falling now; a light, thin wind was blowing out of the lovely stars.

"Beneath my window I saw five persons standing in a little group, all clutching one another like people standing in a flooded river. They were very still; they would not move even when they whispered. As I wondered to see them so fearfully clutching one another a voice spoke in my room:

" 'For God's sake, Stephen, get ready and come down.'

" 'Man, what's the matter with ye?'

" 'For God's sake come down.'

" 'Tell me, tell me!'

" 'How can I? Come down!'

"I tried to be calm; I went out and made for that little group, putting my hand against my eyes, the new snow was so blinding.

" 'Where's the master?' I said.

" 'There!' They did not seem to care whether or not I looked at the master.

"He was a little apart; he was clutching a jut of rock as if the land was slipping from his feet. His cowardice made me afraid. I was hard put to control my breath.

" 'What are ye, are ye all staring at?' I said.

" 'Leaca-na——'—the voice seemed to come from over a mile away, yet it was the man beside me had spoken.

"I looked. The leaca was a dazzling blaze, it was true, but I had often before seen it as bright and wonderful. I was puzzled.

" 'Is it the leaca ye're all staring——' I began; but several of them silently lifted up a hand and pointed towards it. I could have stared at them instead; whether or not it was the white moonlight that was on them, they looked like men half-frozen, too chilled to speak. But I looked where those outstretched hands silently bade me. Then I, too, was struck dumb and became one of that icy group, for I saw a little white cloud moving across the Leaca, a feathery cloud, and from the heart of it there came every now and then a little flash of fire, a spark. Sometimes, too, the little cloud would grow thin, as if it were scattering away, at which times it was a moving shadow we saw. As I blinked at it I felt my hand groping about to catch something, to catch someone, to make sure of myself; for the appearance of everything, the whiteness, the stillness, and then that moving cloud whiter than everything else, whiter than anything in the world, and so like an angel's wing moving along the leaca, frightened me until I felt like fainting away. To make things worse, straight from the little cloud came down a whisper, a long, thin, clear, silvery cry: 'Griosach! Ho-o-o-oh! Ho-o-o-oh!' a ploughing cry. We did not move; we kept our silence: everyone knew that that cry was going through everyone else as through himself, a stroke of coldness. Then I understood why the master was hanging on to a rock; he must have heard the cry before anyone else. It was terrible, made so thin and silvery by the distance; and yet it was a cry of joy—the fool had conquered Griosach!

"I do not know what wild thoughts had begun to come into my head when one man in the group gasped out 'Now!' and then another, and yet another. Their voices were breath, not sound. Then they all said 'Ah!' and I understood the fear that had moved their tongues. I saw the little cloud pause a moment on the edge of the leaca, almost hang over the edge, and then begin to draw back. The fool had turned his team on the vege and was now ploughing up against the hill.

" 'O-o-h,' said the master, in the first moment of relief; it was more like a cry of agony. He looked round at us with ghastly eyes; and our eyeballs turned towards his, just as cold and fixed. Again that silvery cry floated down to us 'Griosach! Ho-o-o-oh!' And again the stroke of coldness passed through every one of us. The cry began to come more frequently, more triumphantly, for now again the little cloud was ploughing down the slope, and its pace had quickened. It was making once more for that edge beneath which was a sheer fall of hundreds of feet.

"Behind us, suddenly, from the direction of the thatched stables came a loud and high whinny—a call to a mate. It was so unexpected, and we were all so rapt up in what was before our eyes, that it shook us, making us spring from one another. I was the first to recover.

" 'My God,' I said, 'that's Niamh, that's Niamh!'

"The whinny came again; it was Niamh surely.

" 'What is he ploughing with, then? What has he with Griosach?'

"A man came running from the stables; he was trying to cry out: he could hardly be heard:

" 'Griosach and Lugh! Griosach and Lugh!'

"Lugh was another sire horse; and the two sires would eat each other; they always had ill-will for each other. The master was staring at us.

" ' 'Tisn't Lugh?' he said, with a gurgle in his voice.

"No one could answer him. We were thinking if the mare's cry reached the sires their anger would blaze up and no one could hold them; but why should Liam have yoked such a team?

" 'Hush! hush!' said a woman's voice.

"We at once heard a new cry; it came down from the leaca:

" 'Griosach, Back! Back!' It was almost inaudible, but we could feel the swiftness and terror in it. 'Back! Back!' came down again. 'Back, Griosach, back!'

"'They're fighting, they're fighting—the sires!' one of our horse-boys yelled out—the first sound above a breath that had come from any of us, for he was fonder of Lugh than of the favourite Griosach, and had forgotten everything else. And we saw that the little cloud was almost at a stand-still; yet that it was disturbed; sparks were flying from it; and we heard little clanking sounds, very faint, coming from it. They might mean great leaps and rearings.

"Suddenly we saw the master spring from that rock to which he had been clinging as limp as a leaf in autumn, spring from it with great life and roar up towards the leaca:

"'Liam! Liam! Liam Ruadh!' He turned to us, 'Shout, boys, and break his fever,' he cried, 'Shout, shout!'

"We were glad of that.

"'Liam! Liam! Liam Ruadh!' we roared.

"'My God! My God!' we heard as we finished. It was the master's voice; he then fell down. At once we raised our voices again; it would keep us from seeing or hearing what was happening on the leaca.

"'Liam! Liam! Liam Ruadh!'

"There was wild confusion.

"'Liam! Liam! Liam! Ruadh! Ruadh! Ruadh!' the mountains were singing back to us, making the confusion worse. We were twisted about—one man staring at the ground, one at the rock in front of his face, another at the sky high over the leaca, and one had his hand stretched out like a sign-post on a hilltop, I remember him best; none of us were looking at the leaca itself. But we were listening and listening, and at last they died, the echoes, and there was a cold silence, cold, cold. Then we heard old Diarmuid's passionless voice begin to pray:

"'*Abhaile ar an sioruidheacht go raibh a anam.*' 'At home in Eternity may his soul——.' We turned round, one by one, without speaking a word, and stared at the leaca. It was